UNDER ANGELS

JACE DANIEL

Under Angels
Copyright © 2012 Jace Daniel. All rights reserved.
Cover design by Jace Daniel.

For more about the author, visit http://jaced.com

ISBN: 1469925230
ISBN-13: 978-1469925233

To Kona and Vive, my friends in darkness.

CONTENTS

PROLOGUE

AFTER THE BOMBING OF PEARL HARBOR in 1941, the threat of a Pacific coastal attack on the United States was real. To prepare for such an attack, the United States designed plans to construct a complex maze of underground tunnels below the city of Los Angeles at Fort MacArthur to sustain critical defenses at the country's largest port.

When the war was over in 1945, all entrances to the tunnels were permanently sealed shut. The perimeter above these entrances remained occupied by the United States Army for decades. With time, the truth about the Los Angeles underground World War II tunnels gradually faded from public memory, and the line between fact and urban legend became blurred.

In 1974, the property above the old Fort MacArthur tunnel entrances was declared surplus land by the United States government. The land was deeded to the City of Los Angeles through the Federal Land to Parks Program.

Eyewitnesses still report sightings of an unidentified man and his dog roaming the area.

CHAPTER ONE

AGAIN. She arched her back on the hard gurney, her bare legs hoisted in the air. Doctors with bloody gloves scrambled as the sound of her pain filled the chamber of concrete walls.

Pete turned and darted out the door, escaping the cold operating room in his lead-soled boots. The damp corridor zigged nowhere in particular, becoming darker with every labored stride, zagging into twisted nothingness. He ran in slow motion through the maze to the cliff's edge, his heartbeat drowning her screams, the rain and Pacific surf pounding the jagged rocks 120 feet below. He finally inhaled --

Pete awoke like a pretzel on the couch, revolver in hand, a string of drool running down his unshaven chin. Salty ocean air and horizontal rays of sunrise barged through the living room curtains.

"I'll be damned."

Cutoff military fatigue pants and a beer-stained ribbed tank top clung to Pete's skin by a clammy musk. He ran his toenails through my coarse hair.

"Consider this, Shadow..."

Pete checked the revolver's chambers. Two bullets left. He spun the cold cylinder with a swipe of his palm, and with a backhanded flick of the wrist, jerked the weapon shut, silencing the clicking buzz with a hard metallic clack.

"Say I had two loaded revolvers," Pete said. "One in each hand. And I held one up to each temple."

Finger on the trigger, Pete stood up and pointed the revolver's barrel to the right side of his skull.

"Do you think I'm good enough to fire both guns simultaneously at the perfect angle to make the bullets collide head-on in the center of my brain?"

BANG. Point blank. The bullet ricocheted off Pete's skull, bouncing off the wall before finding its home in the mess on the floor. Pete dropped the revolver on the coffee table in front of him and fell back onto the couch.

I can't be with her if I can't die.

A laptop computer sat next to the gun on the coffee table. Pete whacked the space bar with his index finger, waking the machine up, numerous web browser windows still covering the screen from the night before. Los Angeles history. World War II blogs. UFO sightings and alien abduction forums. Black magic. Ghost hunts and paranormal reports. Government conspiracy theories. Satanism and the occult. Urban legend fact-checking sites. Quantum physics.

The sound of plastic on wood vibrated from across the room.

"Get my phone, little soldier."

I jumped to my feet and padded across the wood floor, grabbing a scratched cell phone from its usual spot on the credenza next to a framed black-and-white photo of a bride and groom. I padded back to the couch and placed the phone on the crowded coffee table.

Pete picked up the slimy device and read the display:

– – – – –

THE OWL OF GOLD

– – – – –

"*Follow the dog*," Pete mumbled. "Of course. The dog is key."

Pete hit the callback button and held the phone to his ear. It rang twice, and once more --

"Good morning, Sergeant Durante," the voice on the phone scraped.

"*Follow the dog,*" Pete said. "I just need to *follow the dog. The owl of gold, follow the dog --*"

"Meet me at the diner," the voice said. "I have one final key for you."

"When?"

"I'm in our booth now, Sergeant."

Pete tossed the cell phone on the coffee table and stood up from the couch, his thumbs matting his uncut hair behind his ears with its natural grease. His bare feet paced the room of squalor.

"You got something to show me, little soldier?"

We lived in a 1945 California bungalow near the Los Angeles Harbor. A scratched wood floor sprawled through the living room, covered with beer cans, bullet shells, broken razor blades, pencils, magazines, dog toys, and Los Angeles Times crossword puzzles. A foil-wrapped dinner in the corner stopped smelling weeks ago.

"Wait for me here."

Pete grabbed his worn combat boots from the doorway and took a seat on the edge of the couch like a tired boxer between the two final rounds.

"Then you're leading the way."

Pete dug up two random socks from the corners of the couch, pulling them over his feet before slipping into his crusty boots. Leaning, he whispered.

"We're bringing them back."

Besides the faces, the diner hadn't changed in half a century. It was the only one Pete would frequent, walking distance from the house, where the city meets the sea. Open before sunrise, the joint was a breakfast hot-spot for a blue-collar community of fishermen, longshoremen, and construction workers. It always smelled of sausage.

Greamer was lanky and ageless. He sat in the booth closest to the door, dressed down in a black hooded sweatshirt with a black unlabeled baseball cap pulled down low over vaguely shaded thick-rimmed glasses. Stirring black coffee with a knife, he loomed over his handheld device, pushing buttons in a smooth fury.

Pete slid into the old vinyl booth. He breathed through his mouth, looking straight across the table at Greamer, not daring to catch a whiff of the putrid breath he knew too well.

"Tonight you reverse it all, Greamer." Pete pressed his back into the padded booth, trying to gain another inch or two of precious space between himself and Greamer's vileness. "Tonight you bring them back."

"*Man never reverses his choice*, Sergeant." Greamer's abrasive voice was so thick Pete could almost see it.

"Tonight I *follow the dog*," Pete said.

Greamer continued pushing the buttons of his device with indifference, glaring down at his handheld business.

"*The owl of gold*," Pete continued. "*Follow the dog*."

Greamer slapped his hard palm on the table, silverware rattling, coffee splashing on his knuckles. He sneered ugliness, disappointed in himself.

"I can't believe I overlooked the German Shepherd," Greamer said. "Every man loves his dog…"

Greamer shook his head with a flat-coated smile. Pete couldn't even tell where one yellow tooth ended and the next one began.

"Man's best friend," Pete said. "What's this about a final key?"

Greamer wiped the spilled coffee from the tabletop with his sleeve, his sleepless eyes steaming right through Pete. He reached into his pocket and pulled out a sealed envelope.

Branded into the envelope, inkless:

PETER DURANTE

Greamer's bony finger slid the envelope across the table.

"This last key will make sense when you see me again. And you *will* see me again, Sergeant. I assure you."

"Who's giving you these?"

Greamer evaded the question, looking back down at the other business on his device.

"I always admired your *resolve*, Sergeant. Your *journey's key.*"

Greamer tapped the envelope and stood up from the booth, taller than Pete remembered.

"Now if you'll excuse me, Sergeant Durante, I have a design to finish."

And with that, Pete sat alone at the table. He picked up the envelope.

CHAPTER TWO

Closing the front door behind him, Pete sat down on the musty couch and unfolded Greamer's white note, laying it on the coffee table. Other miscellaneous notes loitered all over the room, tacked and taped, scribbled on scraps of paper, napkins, any surface fit for writing on. Even the walls.

Pete's search for the tunnels under Los Angeles started decades earlier, before many men were even born. It was all part of a deal he made with Greamer. Hidden in the tunnels was a special book that Greamer wanted, yet could not find himself. Pete was put in a position to either retrieve the book or suffer great loss.

Pete had combed every corner of the city using every resource available: public records, newspaper clippings, history books, maps, conversations with eyewitnesses, websites. Greamer would regularly drip-feed Pete new keys, and seemed to find delight in his failure to find the hidden entrance to the subterranean complex.

"He wants to play with the Enigma again, little soldier."

Pete swiped bullet shells off the coffee table with his forearm, his tarred thumbs rubbing out the two neat creases of Greamer's last key. Final instructions. Inkless, yet readable:

- - - - -

Read Instructions. Enigma.

Just

Know

Man

Never

Reverses

His

Choice.

Resolve,

His

Journey's

Key.

— — — — —

"Journey's key. Choice..."

Still in his boots, Pete stood from the couch and walked across the room to review dozens of other crisp white notes tacked to the wall. A tapestry of Greamer's keys, collected and deciphered over the years. Each key held a set of words, often with curious punctuation and arrangement, with a sordid riddling style. Individual puzzles in a larger game of wordplay. Often nonsensical, but never without meaning.

Pete spoke aloud, reading from the wall's top layer of tacked notes for the billionth time.

"Turn repeated. Do over..."

"Coast still. Defense. Batteries included..."

"Home gunning can. On sweet home. Protection..."

"Soft nuke debacle. Beacon dusk Fleet. Fueled on setback..."

"Lookout on your watch..."

Pete punched the wall and walked to the couch.

"*The owl of gold*, little soldier. That's it. *Follow the dog*. You're the key."

Pete sat on the floor beside me.

"You ready to get your nose into some weird shit? You'll be my eyes and ears down there tonight."

I was ready for the mission.

Pete had uncovered conflicting theories about the tunnels over the years, ranging from slightly peculiar to utterly bizarre. Some sources suspected a Cold War government conspiracy, with underground passages crawling all the way up to Malibu. Some believed the tunnels concealed extraterrestrial secrets. Other sources believed satanic groups used the facilities to perform animal sacrifices, with several experts identifying the labyrinth as a fertile bed for the paranormal. There's never been a shortage of ghostly sightings along the Los Angeles coasts and around its lighthouses.

"I'm putting you on point, little soldier."

Pete grabbed my chin and looked me in the eyes.

"You got a problem with that?"

Nope.

"I didn't think so." Pete scratched my ears. "My little soldier of darkness --"

KNOCK-KNOCK-KNOCK

The front door shook with three persistent thumps. Pete's hand froze, his glazed eyes locked on mine. Concerned. We never had visitors during the day.

14

"Who is it, little soldier?"

And again.

KNOCK-KNOCK-KNOCK-KNOCK-KNOCK

Louder. I just wagged my tail.

Pete grabbed the revolver from the coffee table and opened the chamber. One bullet left. Scooping up a handful of loose bullets from the table, he loaded the weapon with five more.

"What are you, deaf?"

Deaf? Far from it. I can hear everything Pete hears, I can sense everything he senses. Tenfold. I know everything he's thinking, now and forever. It's one of the secret skills we dogs have. Our labor of love.

Pete got up and walked to the front door. He hesitated as the knocks continued in a relentless encore.

KNOCK-KNOCK-KNOCK-KNOCK-KNOCK --

"Who is it?"

"Sent by Rip Greamer."

The voice out on the porch was deep. Urban mashed up with a southern drawl.

Greamer?

Pete turned the knob and swung the door open.

"Excuse me, brother..."

A man stepped through the doorway, lumbering past Pete and into the living room toward me. It was the same man who took my mother a long time ago. I hadn't seen him since the night I was born.

"Shadow." The man crouched down to the floor with a friendly growl. "How ya doin', Lucky Thirteen? I knew you'd be a big one, brother."

"What is this?" Pete said, spooked by the combination of the man's forwardness and my silence.

"Check you out, Lucky Thirteen!" The man scratched his unclipped fingernails on my upturned belly. "Kick that leg, dog. You like that, don'tcha?"

Do you have to ask?

Pete stood over us, nudging the man's hand away from me with his combat boot. For the first time in my life, Pete felt like I was out of his control.

"Little soldier?" Pete asked, stupefied. "What the --"

The man wore scrubs from the waist down and an old knit poncho with no sleeves, revealing a dirty cast on his left wrist and a tattoo of two black wings on his right arm. He smelled like sweet smoke. I lay on my back as he got to his feet and held out his leathery hand.

"Name's Mag, brother."

Standing a foot taller than Pete and outweighing him by a hundred pounds of solid muscle, Mag looked about ten years past his prime. He exuded a youthful spirit with a hard wisdom lurking behind bloodshot eyes.

"Mag," Pete said. "That short for Magnus? Magnum?"

"Whatever you want it to be, brother."

"How do you know Greamer?" Pete asked.

Pete kept his hands at his sides. He had never met another person in recent years who knew Greamer, nor had he ever spoken of their meetings. The fact that Mag knew Greamer's name made Pete nervous.

"I'm just a subcontractor, brother," Mag said. "Extra work."

"Any friend of Greamer's is no friend of mine."

Mag laughed. Despite his dominating physical presence, he had a playful, almost childlike smile, riddled with missing teeth and fillings.

"Rip ain't no friend, brother. He done me wrong from jump street. Always sticking me with the dirty jobs."

"Then why do you work for him?"

"He owes me," said Mag. "Can't quit without getting paid, you know? Matter of fact, the son of a bitch already stiffed me over a hundred times. Over a hundred times, brother."

Pete bit his lip.

"What's he got you working on?"

"This, that, and the other thing. It's all numbers with Rip."

And letters. "Who does Greamer work for?" Pete asked.

"Rip can't never talk about that, brother."

Mag laughed. Pete had hit on a subject that was off limits.

"As long as he makes quota, it's all good," Mag said. "I just round 'em up 'til sunrise. Then I do it all over again."

"Sunrise?"

"Sunrise is when they gotta be in. Got just this one stop today."

Pete walked to the front window, gun in hand. Pulling the curtains aside a few inches, he peered outside, looking for others.

"One stop," Pete said. "You alone?"

Mag smiled. "Always alone."

"And I'm your stop." Pete pulled the curtains shut. "Did he tell you about her?"

Mag looked at Shadow.

"About who, brother?"

"Do you know where the book is?"

Mag was confused.

"I don't know about no book, brother. I'm just the delivery man. Here to pick up the soul."

Pete looked around the room, the walls lined with Greamer's notes, tacked and taped. His stare stopped on a large map of Los Angeles, tacked to the wall, a single red pushpin marking a possible location of the tunnel entrance.

It's over. I got close enough. Greamer has sent for me.

"Then my soul is ready." Pete tucked the gun in the waist of his cutoffs and grabbed my leash from the credenza.

Mag scratched his head.

"Sorry, brother. Dang. I don't think you understand."

Pete faced Mag.

"My dog goes where I go," Pete said. "He's coming with us. I'm not leaving him here."

19

Mag shrugged. Apologetic.

"You don't understand, brother. I ain't here for you."

The words hit Pete like a sledgehammer to the groin. He didn't need an explanation, but Mag explained anyway.

"I'm here to pick up Shadow."

CHAPTER THREE

I LOVE A GOOD GHOST STORY. Those tales of lost souls stuck between life and death, with unfinished business, unable to rest in peace. Like the little girl who drowned in the well a hundred years ago, whom people still claim to see skipping rope in the garden. Or the woman in white who's been walking around the lighthouse for years, waiting for her lover to return home from sea. It's as if all these ghosts are suspended in some kind of perpetual cycle, caught in a loop, doing the same thing night after night. This is a story about one of them.

I was born in Los Angeles. We have a haunted Army base here known as Fort MacArthur. Maybe you've heard of it. Constructed back in 1914 during the military buildup surrounding World War I, its massive guns could shoot a shell as heavy as a Volkswagen Bug over fourteen miles. But for two decades, the cannons of Fort Mac were silent.

Then came the attack on Pearl Harbor. At the time, it was the worst attack ever on American soil, and its implications were terrifying. If the Japanese could take out the Los Angeles Harbor, the results would be devastating for the *entire country*. The Pearl Harbor attack effectively put the United States, Los Angeles, and Fort Mac in the middle of a world war, and our city became the national nerve center for a possible all-out battle for the Pacific.

Fear was at an all-time high. With enemy submarines lurking just off our shores, the United States constructed a top-secret labyrinth of tunnels beneath our city to brace for an enemy attack. Most people don't know about the World War II tunnels under Los Angeles. And the folks who do know? They never talk about it.

But I'm getting ahead of myself. Allow me to start from the beginning. My beginning, anyway.

My father's name was Dash. A black-and-tan German Shepherd just over fifty pounds, he wasn't the biggest dog Pete had ever trained, but he was the best, paws down. Recognized for his valiant service to our nation in time of war, Dad was declared a K-9

Veteran of World War II and buried in our cemetery with the highest of honors.

Sitting on a dark drizzly hillside near Fort Mac, Pete finished a Los Angeles Times crossword puzzle under the light of his headlamp and stuffed it into a rucksack full of other crossword puzzles, all solved. Dad sat by his side. It was September of 1939, almost two and a half years before I was born.

Wearing Army field gear under an issued trench coat, Pete examined a woman's ring that had been shoved tightly on his pinky. A plain gold band, custom, with letters engraved around the circumference: *DREAM TURNS*. Pete showed the dog the ring.

"See it yet? *Dream turns*. Rearrange the letters, Dash. It's *Mrs. Durante*. Keep up with me here, soldier..."

In addition to its anti-aircraft gunning stations and other military facilities, Fort Mac served as the location for the United States Army's K-9 Command Unit, a program designed to train dogs for war. Sergeant Peter Durante trained many of us, including my parents.

Pete and Dad were assigned to each other in the K-9 Command Unit, spending every hour of their shifts together, training Dad for combat situations. It wasn't an easy program, and only the very best of us had what it took to graduate. And, luckily for me, they didn't fix the good ones.

Like all K-9 man-dog teams, Dad and Pete were put on rigorous 24-hour shifts, from midnight to midnight, occasionally stringing two or even three shifts together one after another for extra conditioning. This demanding schedule, designed to mimic the unpredictable and unforgiving conditions of war, made it impossible to sync up with the sun and settle into a regular sleep routine. So catching a nap whenever and wherever you could was a necessary skill.

The job of these two-soul teams here at home was to patrol the coastal perimeter of the Los Angeles Harbor area at night, on foot, with important combat training exercises during the day. Pete's job as a dog handler was to prepare Dad for the worst, and they both took their job very seriously. Once they were done working together and said their goodbyes, Dad had to be ready for anything. Our boys over there weren't playing games.

Pete stood to his feet on the damp hillside.

"Damn it --"

Pete's arm flailed, shaking off an earthworm clinging to the cuff of his trench coat's sleeve. When it came to worms, or larvae, or any kind of subterranean life form, he became like a queasy little girl.

"Son of a bitch."

Pete picked up his rucksack and grabbed his canteen.

"Bottom's up, soldier." Pete took a knee and gave Dad a swig of water in his cupped hand. "Tomorrow's the big day. Keep your paws crossed for me..."

The two went pee and embarked on the misty two-mile night prowl back to the main base. Making their way down a muddy hillside, they reached the paved coastline road and walked in a disciplined straight line along the dark bluff.

"She's as good as they get..."

Dad walked at Pete's left in heel position, patiently listening to the same story for the hundredth time that day. Spending dozens of consecutive hours together creates a bond between a man and a dog that can't be fully explained in words. Pete would tell Dad things that he'd never tell anybody.

"Think she'll say yes?"

My Dad was a German Shepherd, but our troops came to the fort from various families including Doberman Pinschers, Rottweilers, retrievers, Chow mixes, Schnauzers, various terriers, Cocker Spaniels, and bulldog half-breeds. At the onset of World War II and immediately after the attack on Pearl Harbor, hundreds of us would be volunteered for war duty by Los Angeles citizens in response to radio calls and newspaper announcements.

Some of us that were trained at Fort MacArthur throughout the years had been smart enough to get out of war duty, finding fame in Hollywood. Terry, a female Cairn Terrier, was recruited to play Toto in the movie *The Wizard of Oz*. Another one of us, Buck, was used as one of the dogs in Jack London's *The Call of the Wild*. And a German Shepherd named Rin, the grandson of Rin-Tin-Tin, was one of the smartest to ever come out of our camp.

With the rocky coastal bluffs just a few hundred yards away, Pete and Dad entered the unlit upper reservation and walked across the slick courtyard, ducking into the entrance of a large concrete military facility dug into a hillside called a battery. Our batteries were equipped with heavy artillery to protect our beaches from intruders.

"Let's get you tucked in."

Fort Mac was typically pretty quiet by midnight, with most of the activity occurring during the daytime hours. But on this night, the halls smelled like freshly brewed coffee, with loud arguing adult voices coming from a brightly lit office just inside the battery entrance.

"What do you suppose is going on in there, Dash?"

Pete and Dad passed by the office door, walking to the end of the battery's hall to the K-9 barracks where they'd kennel us in between shifts. Nodding to the boyish kennel guard, Pete opened the latch to the gate of Dad's kennel containing a modest cot, an empty metal bowl for the next morning's hearty meal, and a large metal bucket of fresh water that never went empty. Pete dropped his rucksack to the floor and hung the leash.

"Rest up, soldier. I'll see you at zero hundred."

Pete closed the latch of Dad's kennel as another trainer's voice echoed from down the hall.

"Jackson, *vamanos mi primo...*"

It was Vasquez, suited up in dry dungarees and carrying a rucksack. On his left walked his partner Jackson, another German Shepherd. Vasquez and Jackson -- K-9 61 -- were just about to begin their 24-hour shift, taking over where Pete and Dad had left off.

"Nobody gets through on our watch," Vasquez said. "Not through *sesenta y uno...*"

Jackson was another one of the best. He and Dad both entered the war dog platoon the same summer, immediately placed in the training unit of aggressive dog soldiers to be used as weapons of war. The job demanded that they were physically fit, responsive to voice commands, not gun-shy, and able to stand their ground against assailants without cowering. Dogs that made the K-9 unit were the elite, like royalty, and treated with the highest priority. If Pete and Dad were out in the hills and Pete got bitten by a rattlesnake, they'd drive him to the hospital. If Dad got bitten, they'd fly in a helicopter. A fallen war dog would be a significant loss of resources.

"Durante," Vasquez said. "Did you hear?"

Vasquez and Pete slapped hands up high.

"Hear what?" Pete asked.

"Shit just hit the fan today, amigo. Hitler's invaded Poland."

"Fuck..."

Our world had become a scary, unpredictable place, with threats of evil gradually making themselves known all around the globe. How exactly the United States was to fit into things was not yet clear.

"Is that what's going on in Briefing Quarters?" Pete asked. "There must be half a dozen people in there. I saw civilians too."

"We got a message from the Brits," Vasquez said. "Intercepted from the Nazis. It's encrypted."

"The voices I heard were American."

"Brits wired it this morning," Vasquez said. "Parallel intel's looking at it now. Black Chamber rounded up some crypto experts from other parts of the city."

We would soon learn that there were some very bad people in Europe, led by a tyrant with plans to systematically execute a certain group of people. Entire families were being torn apart, their dogs left on the streets to starve. Men, women, and children were being destroyed in ovens, the fillings from their teeth removed, their skin used for lampshades, all for something these bad people considered the final solution to a problem. It's a problem I'll never understand.

"Is Naylor in there?" Pete asked.

"Yeah." Vasquez looked at his watch. "We're on, Jackson. Time to protect the world, *mi primo*."

Pete walked with Vasquez and Jackson down the hard hall, stopping outside the lit office as the two headed out into the wet night.

"Go get 'em, Sixty-one," Pete said. "See you on the other side." *And look out for things that wiggle and slither.*

Pete stopped at the office door and peered inside. Voices still shouted amongst themselves, involved in some sort of collaborative debate.

"I still think it's *U.S.* something," a voice said. "*U.S. dog line den.* Or *God line den --*"

"*U.S. long denied*," another voice interrupted.

"*Sledged union*," said another. "It's the Soviets."

"*Dungeon slide*," said another.

The hell? Curious, Pete stepped closer to the door as a hand tapped him on the shoulder. Startled, Pete turned around to see a young fellow swimming in a mess of wrinkled corduroy and chomping the last of an apple. His caffeinated eyes peered through spectacles a half inch thick.

"You looking for the crypto meeting?" the young man said.

"Huh?"

"Hitler invaded Poland today."

"Yeah, I heard..."

"Come on," the young man said. "We're late. I'm Charlie."

"Pete."

Pete and Charlie stepped into an office cramped with about eight people, all men and one woman, some with notepads. Among them was Naylor, Pete's commanding officer. They were all studying two words written boldly in chalk on a blackboard:

SLEDGED UNION

Naylor greeted Pete with his eyes and turned to a fat man in a beige suit.

"He works with the dogs," Naylor said. "But he eats crossword puzzles like potato chips."

Naylor turned to Pete and pointed to the blackboard.

"Whaddya make of this, Durante? Show us your stuff."

A baggy-eyed bald man in a plain white shirt and slacks chewed the eraser off the end of a pencil, looking down at his notepad. "*Dodge sun line*. It'll be something at night. I also have *delousing den* --"

"*Lunged on side*," an elderly man in a plaid flannel shirt said, not noticing Pete. "Or *sudden legion*. I still see *sudden legion*. Timing..."

"*Sledged union?*" Pete whispered.

"Anagram," Charlie said. "Mixed message."

The room studied the board in mumbling silence, scratching down notes.

"Why would it be in English?" Pete whispered.

Charlie nodded, pointing to the room, motioning for Pete to chime in. Pete gazed at the two words on the board.

SLEDGED UNION

Pete turned to the people and spoke up, pointing to the blackboard. "What if it's missing an umlaut?"

Stares stuck to Pete like magnets as he walked across the room to the blackboard. He picked up a piece of chalk and added two dots over the letter *O*. An umlaut.

SLEDGED UNIÖN.

"That's what I was saying," said the woman in the corner. "I suspect it's Germanic. Perhaps even Icelandic or Swedish."

Pete stood at the blackboard like an instructor in front of a stumped class. The fat man in the beige suit broke the awkward silence, holding a slip of paper.

"Sergeant...?"

"Durante," Pete finished. "Pete Durante. K-9 Fifty-three. I handle Dash."

"Sergeant Durante," the beige-suited fat man continued. "We suspect this is a transposition cipher of some sort. Do you know what an anagram is, Sergeant?"

"Of course."

"Can you make anything of that?"

Pete stared at the blackboard, calculating.

SLEDGED UNIÖN

Pete closed his eyes and concentrated. Letting his mind fly, letting the chalked words sear into his imagination.

SLEDGED UNIÖN

Pete rearranged the letters in his head, paying close attention to the Ö.

"The first thing I see is *die*," Pete said, opening his eyes. "*D-I-E*. German for *the*. *Die* something..."

SLEDGED UNIÖN. Pete looked at the shapes of the letters, fantasizing, shifting them upside-down and sideways in his mind. He flipped them over each other, stacking them, rolling them back and forth, shuffling them, picking them up in his hands, shaking them, tossing them in the air to let them fall where they may, looking at the results. What probably should've been difficult to see became obvious to him, zooming from the blackboard into his consciousness.

"*Endlösung.*"

The word spilled from Pete's mouth, pronounced with an authentically learned accent.

"*Die Endlösung. Sledged union* is an anagram for *die Endlösung.*"

The room fell silent.

Pete grabbed a piece of chalk and wrote two words in all caps on the available space of the blackboard:

DIE ENDLÖSUNG

Pete stepped back from the blackboard and read it to himself.

SLEDGED UNIÖN
DIE ENDLÖSUNG

"*Solution*," Pete said out loud. "*The final solution.*"

Pete wrote three English words on the available space of the board.

THE FINAL SOLUTION

"*The final solution*," Pete repeated, stepping back. "*Die Endlösung* is German for *the final solution.* Does that mean anything to anybody? *The final solution*?"

Blank stares. The beige-suited fat man walked to the blackboard, taking the chalk from Pete's hand.

"Sergeant Durante, I take it you're stationed here at Fort MacArthur?"

"K-nine Fifty-three. Dash."

The beige-suited fat man nodded, looking around the room of fatigued eyes.

"Are you familiar with encryption, Sergeant?"

"A little," Pete said. "Just from puzzles and such."

"Have you ever worked with machines?"

"Machines?"

"Encryption machines."

"No."

Naylor laughed. "He just takes crossword puzzles into the shitter three at a time."

The beige-suited fat man put his hand on Pete's shoulder.

"Sergeant Durante, we have a special project for you."

CHAPTER FOUR

FRIEND [FREND] *n.* 1. one to whom another is attached by feelings of affection or trust. 2. one to whom another gives support, sympathy, or assistance. 3. one with whom another is allied in a struggle or cause; a comrade.

Mag took a knee and scratched his nails under my chin like a rake. All business, he spoke with the muted emotion of a proficient coroner on a routine errand. In no hurry, and not particularly fond of his job.

"It's Shadow's time, brother. Rip needs him before sunrise."

Pete clicked his mouth for me, his calloused fingertips twitching against his thumb. With one snap of his fingers, the command came.

Take Mag out. "On your feet, little soldier. Get him."

The command fell flat.

"Ain't no use, brother." Mag laughed, unsurprised. "The dog knows why I'm here. He won't resist me. He can't. It's his time."

What the hell is going on here? Stripped of his greatest weapon, Pete grabbed the revolver from the waist of his cutoffs.

"You ain't gotta do that, brother."

"I can't let you take my dog," Pete said.

Mag lounged into the couch, his woody toenails pressing up against the underside of the coffee table. He grunted a tired sigh, like an overworked courier sneaking in a five-minute break in the middle of a long day.

"Afraid I have to, brother. Quota."

Pete stood in the middle of the room and held the gun out at arm's length, pointing it at Mag's face.

"Get up, motherfucker."

Mag rolled his eyes and shook his head.

"Go stand by the door," Pete ordered, both hands on the gun. "I don't want blood on her couch."

Mag stood up, smiling his metal-toothed grin, his shins bumping into the coffee table. Staring down the barrel of the gun, he held his arms out at his sides, palms up.

"Brother, I'm telling you --"

Point blank three times twice, emptying the chambers. The bullets thudded into Mag's chest like marbles hitting a pillow before falling to join the mess on the floor.

What the goddamn --

Pete dropped the revolver and shouted.

"Who the hell are you?"

"I'm just the delivery man, brother. Here to pick up Lucky Thirteen."

Unfazed, Mag sat back down on the couch and looked around the room at the notes and memoirs covering the walls. His eyes stopped on the tattered map of Los Angeles, tacked to the far wall at all four corners, a single red pushpin puncturing the region near the lower left.

"What's all this stuff for?"

"Greamer and I have some unfinished business," Pete said. He had surrendered. "I need to find him something hidden in the tunnels. You know how to get in?"

"Nah," Mag said. "Rip don't tell me jack."

Mag's foot twitched, a cell phone vibrating against his leg in the loose pocket of his scrubs. Leaning back into the couch, he pulled the phone out, checked the display, and quickly pocketed it again. He leaned forward and picked up Greamer's note from the coffee table.

"This from Rip?"

"Crypto." Pete paced the room.

"Like secret code?"

"Something like that."

Pete pulled out his cell phone and pulled up Greamer's text. Holding the phone out, he showed Mag the display.

"*The owl of gold*?"

"*Follow the dog*," Pete said. "Rearrange the letters. It's a transposition cipher. An anagram. A key. Shadow's my way in."

"Rip wrote you that?"

"He got it from somebody bigger," Pete said. "Maybe his boss. Or maybe he intercepted it. I don't really know."

Mag pointed to the wall of notes.

"Those from Rip too?"

"Yeah." Pete burped the smell of sour beer. "Greamer's been forwarding me these keys to crack a puzzle he can't solve himself. He must have missed the point of the dog. The dog is the key to the tunnels. That's where the book is."

Taking a knee beside me, Pete rolled my ears in his fingers like velvet triangles, rubbing his thumb firmly and comfortably between my eyes. We stared at each other.

"I need Shadow tonight, Mag. I won't let you take him."

Mag walked to the map of Los Angeles on the adjacent wall, the heels of his loose sandals dragging across the wood floor. Crossing his arms across his chest, he studied the map's wrinkled surface, silently reading its labels. He pointed to the red pushpin.

"*L-thirteen*," Mag said, reading the coordinates from the map.

Pete clambered to his feet and joined Mag at the map.

"What?"

"*L-thirteen*," Mag repeated, pointing to the red pushpin, its coordinates at *L-13*. "You marked it. *L* here and *thirteen* here."

Pete looked at the ceiling.

"How do you know my dog, Mag? How do you know Shadow?"

"We go way back, brother. Night I picked up his twelve brothers and sisters… and their mama. Shadow was the sole survivor. The *soul* survivor, brother. Lucky Thirteen."

"Lucky Thirteen." Pete pointed to the red pushpin. "*L-thirteen*. Explain that."

Mag's neck straightened.

Pete turned from the wall and walked back to the window, peeking out the curtains.

"What does Greamer do with the souls after you turn them in, Mag?"

"After?" Mag scratched his scalp. "Says it ain't my business. Ain't no business of mine."

Pete pulled the curtains tight. *This guy doesn't trust his boss. He's curious.*

"You seem afraid of him."

Mag turned from the map and shrugged.

"Quota, brother. Rip'll cut me off if I don't make the quota."

"You said he expects you at sunrise? Tomorrow?"

"Sunrise, yeah. That's when they gotta be in."

"Then we have all night."

Pete stepped away from the window.

"Tonight we get back what he owes me," Pete said. "Some unfinished business we have."

"Owes you?" Mag looked confused.

"You're not the only one he's ripped off. He took my wife. If I don't find him the *Triad of Hell*, he'll keep her forever."

Pete kicked the revolver across the floor. Mag pointed to the framed photo on the credenza.

"That's her, huh, brother? They don't make 'em like that anymore. You musta loved her."

"*Triad of Hell*. Forever."

"*Triad of Hell*, brother?"

"It's a code book," Pete said.

"The code book?" Mag looked interested. "*Theee* code book?"

"What do you know about it?"

"I told you Rip don't tell me jack."

Pete looked around the room. "It'll be dark soon. I need to sack up some gear in the garage. Shit I'll need once I'm in."

Pete leaned over the coffee table and picked up Greamer's note. He folded it and stuffed it into his pocket.

"I'm taking my dog, Mag. You can't stop me. I need him."

Mag rubbed his eyes and contemplated.

"Alright then, brother. *Follow the dog.* But I'm going with you."

"My dog and I work alone," Pete said. "As a unit."

Mag snapped.

"Whaddya want me throw the dog in the van now, brother?"

"Fair enough. Let's sack up some shit."

CHAPTER FIVE

HOUR BEFORE DARK. The late afternoon sun ran across the dead backyard lawn and crashed into a detached garage that could have used a paint job decades ago. Pete fought with a rusted latch and pulled up the large door, the smell of sawdust and rotting cardboard escaping out to the cracked cement driveway.

"Haven't been out here in ages," Pete said.

A makeshift woodshop, with old military gear occupying most of the garage's corners. Rifles and parachutes, mosquito nets and Army helmets, ammo cans and dead grenades. Burlap duffel bags and canvas utility pouches hung from nails hammered into bare-framed walls. A faded green tarp covered the window, tacked up like a curtain. Sawdust everywhere.

Mag dropped his cell phone into the pocket of his scrubs and waded into the sea of clutter.

"You hiding a battleship in here or something, brother?"

Pete pulled the tarp from the window, allowing the sunlight in from the west. A rope dangled from the ceiling's rafters, seven feet above an overturned unfinished chair, its frayed silhouette finding a dusty blackboard on the east wall of the garage.

Mag pointed to a dismantled machine, about the size of a typewriter, sitting on the sawdust-covered workbench.

"What's that?"

Laid out like a radio halfway through an autopsy, the contraption was a hybrid of mechanical and electrical systems, with a keyboard and a series of rotating disks arranged adjacently along a spindle. A layer of dust covered the exposed electrical circuit board and its tangled mess of spliced wires.

"Enigma machine," Pete said. "For a project we called *Ultra* in Europe."

Mag examined the machine without touching it.

"Enigma. Like on Rip's note?"

"Axis messaging system," Pete said. "We cracked it. Poles got to it first. Brits couldn't keep up after the

Germans upgraded to four rotors, so they sent it over here for a few of us to reverse-engineer."

"How'd you do it?"

Pete reached up and pulled down two large olive-drab rucksacks from the rafters.

"A few of us used the Adam and Eve prototypes after Poland gave us the head start. It was a dinosaur by the time we got it. Nazis were too busy acting like assholes to notice we were onto them."

Pete pounded his palms into the empty rucksacks, shaking out the dust.

"They upgraded it before the war, but it still had flaws. Weak. Lucky for us, the fools kept broadcasting the dates and locations of their attacks. It was like taking candy from a baby."

Pete motioned to a tall stack of boxes in the corner.

"Get the headlamps. One of the boxes."

Mag slid a large cardboard box off the top of the stack and tossed it to the floor. An airy lace wedding dress, yellowing with age, poured from the box. Setting a bayonet aside, he fumbled through another box and grabbed a canteen with a pair of night-vision goggles.

"And the grappling hooks," Pete mumbled. "Bottom box."

Pete sifted through a rack of neatly hung clothing and pulled out a WWII-era Army trench coat, a pair of military fatigue pants, and an olive-drab assault vest loaded with pockets. Setting the ensemble on the workbench, he unhung two long coils of rope from the wood-framed wall and packed them into one of the rucksacks. Two folded shovels followed.

"Yo --"

Mag held a grappling hook wrapped in a length of rope.

"Go long, brother."

Pete caught the grappling hook and stuffed it into the rucksack.

"And these..."

Mag pulled out two miner flashlights mounted on elastic head straps and tossed them across the garage. The two worked the garage like a basketball court, passing pieces of gear around like a rehearsed offense. Mag serving up the assists, Pete dunking the pieces into the rucksacks.

Pete bagged a large flashlight and took inventory.

"Okay," Pete said. *Shovels, hooks, rope, crowbar, knives, lights.* "We're good."

"The lights still work, brother?"

"Just need to pick up batteries."

Mag pushed the looted boxes aside with his feet and walked to a pile of printed documents and newspapers in the back of the garage. He knelt and picked up the top document, skimming over its faded copy.

"What's the Black Chamber, brother?"

Pete pulled Greamer's note from the pocket of his cutoffs.

"Cipher Bureau. Before the N.S.A."

Dropping his cutoffs to his ankles, Pete slipped into the vest and shoved Greamer's note into the chest pocket.

"Black Chamber was our first crypto organization. Intel for the Department of Defense."

Pete stepped into the dusty fatigues and pulled them up over his boxer shorts.

"Black Chamber," Mag said. "Anything to do with the *Triad of Hell*?"

"I don't know yet."

Mag flipped through tattered newspapers in the stack, reading headlines in his deep understated grunt.

"*Anti-aircraft guns blast at L.A. mystery invader... Army says alarm real... What to do in an air raid... Purple?*"

Mag looked up and pointed to the blackboard. Four columns remained scribbled on it from decades earlier, with large headers chalked across the top.

RED CORAL JADE PURPLE

Written beneath each header, like a list, was a column of vertically arranged Oriental characters.

"*Purple*," Mag repeated, pulling a brown shabby newspaper from the pile. "Japanese?"

"Yep."

Mag walked to the blackboard and ran his fingertip down the hashed Oriental characters in the *PURPLE* column.

"What's this all mean?"

Pete tucked his pants into his boots.

"Secret instructions from the Japanese commander. Yamamoto. For his pawns. Only they weren't so secret after we cracked Purple."

Pete walked to the blackboard and pointed to a character near the bottom.

"This one here was their big fuck-up. Told us the lowest naval ratio acceptable to Tokyo. We gave it to our negotiators to push the Japs to it after Midway."

Pete strode back to the workbench and hopped up, standing on its surface. He reached up with both arms and pulled another machine off the top shelf.

Jumping back down to the floor, he held the machine in his hands like an accordion.

"This is the rig they used. Stepping switches instead of half-rotor switches. We called it Purple."

Mag examined the machine in Pete's arms.

"More secure than the Red machine," Pete explained. "But they didn't know we already cracked Red. We lucked out."

Pete checked out the machine's switchboard like an enthusiastic old man remembering one of his boyhood train sets.

"Purple inherited a weakness from Red," Pete continued. "A vowel-consonant separate encryption. We called it *sixes-twenties*."

Pete swiped his forearm across the surface of the workbench, loose items flying into the forgotten crevices of the cluttered garage. He put the Purple machine on the workbench next to the Enigma.

"Then we gave the bastards a taste of their own poison and they ran off with their tails between their legs. For a while, anyway."

Pete grabbed a compass from the shelf, tucked it into a vest pocket, and threw on the trench coat. He looked out at me lying on the driveway.

"I need to go online before we split. And I need to charge my phone. Then we need to pick up some batteries. Then we *follow the dog.*"

Mag picked up both packed rucksacks and swung them over his two broad shoulders. He walked out to the driveway as Pete closed the garage door behind them.

"So, hey, brother..."

Pete latched the door and turned from the garage.

"Yeah?"

Mag set the rucksacks down on the driveway next to me.

"What happened to her?"

CHAPTER SIX

IT STARTED ON the organ's cue. Pete stood groping it in his pocket, still warm, delivered under his door that morning. Her letter. Two words: *CAN'T WAIT.* The small crowd of witnesses stood politely for a piece of forever as she walked the final steps with her father, fiery locks ushering eyes of ice behind a steaming white veil. She winked. Pete couldn't hold back his smile. He saw her laugh silently.

It all felt like a dream, and it smelled like roses.

CHAPTER SEVEN

THE DESOLATE PARKING LOT of a supermarket open later than everything else. I waited with the rucksacks in Mag's van, kept company by the smells of stale leaf smoke and spilled coffee. It wasn't more than a few minutes before three stinky men walked purposefully across the parking lot and entered the store through its sliding glass doors.

"Figures," Pete said. "Everything but batteries."

Pete and Mag perused Aisle 9 in the back of the uncrowded supermarket near the fresh meats. Like two rats from a pirate ship raiding a junk drawer, they rummaged through racks and shelves of boxed light bulbs, packaged padlocks, extension cords and power strips, egg timers, masking tape, motor oil, pot holders, scissors, and tin foil.

"Prolly up front by the register, brother --"

POP- POP-

Curdled screams came from the front of the store, punctuated by gunshots. Pete's eyes locked on Mag's.

POP-

A child bawled beneath the sounds of adult shouts and screams. A male's angry voice resounded louder than the others.

POP- POP-

Three workers in aprons and name tags scurried like startled cats from the front counters, sprinting down the aisles to the back of the store. A heavyset manager with a mustache and wire-framed glasses barreled down Aisle 9 past Pete and Mag.

"The back," he babbled in a panic. "The back! The freezer! The back! Hurry --"

The clatter of deadly commotion persisted at the front of the supermarket, the child's high-pitched hysteria mixed with grown male shouts.

"OPEN IT!!!"

Lips shut, Pete held up a fist and pointed to his eyes with fingers in a *V*. In a simplified form of sign language, he instructed Mag to go to the back of Aisle 9, down and around to the end of the butcher counter toward the breads, and circle back up to the front of the store from the produce section at the east wall. Mag disappeared without a word as the noise continued at the front of the store.

Pete took stealthy strides up Aisle 9 to the front of the supermarket toward the chaos. The angry male's words were clear enough to hear above the child's unending screams.

"OPEN IT, BITCH!!!"

Another male voice, soft-spoken and anxious, pleaded.

"I... don't even work here --"

"OPEN THE COMPUTER!!!"

"It's not... it's not a computer --"

Pete reached the front end of Aisle 9 unnoticed, peering around the corner of a display of soda pop. He looked at what was happening at Register 4.

"OPEN THE COMPUTER OR I'LL CAP YOUR ASS!!!"

A delicate man with jet black hair stood behind the counter at Register 4 with his hands up, his head held at sloppy gunpoint by a stinky man in loose clothes that were way too warm for the evening. The stinky gunman's two friends stood at the two front doors watching the parking lot.

Pete's eyes scrubbed the front of the supermarket. *What the hell is going on here?*

A toddler curled himself up against the store's front wall of batteries, sobbing in what had become a tired moan. A nervous woman, talkative and in shock, stood between the child and the stinky gunman at Register 4. She moved forward, arguing.

"He doesn't even work here --"

"SHUT YOUR FUCKING KID UP!!!"

The stinky gunman turned with elbow out, backhanding his forearm across the woman's jaw with a muted crack. She crumpled to the floor next to the toddler, its lungs empty of screams.

"BITCH!!!"

The stinky gunman turned back to the register, pointing his semi-automatic pistol back at the delicate man. Behind the counter lay a store clerk. A woman, mid-fifties, shot thrice, bleeding. The delicate man stood over her, his hands in the air, his eyes closed, shaking his head. He turned to face the stinky gunman.

"Please --"

"OPEN THE COMPUTER!!!"

The stinky gunman held out his pistol stiff-armed like a thug, sideways.

"I... I can't think --"

"OPEN IT, BITCH!!!"

Pete spoke up.

"Leave him alone."

Pete walked past the racked magazines and breath mints at the closed Express Lane at Register 1. Grabbing an empty shopping cart from the open floor, he rolled it in front of the woman and child and stood facing Register 4.

"Where do you get off threatening a man and harming his family?" Pete asked.

"BACK OFF, BITCH!!!"

The stinky gunman held the weapon with both hands, pointing it at Pete, not noticing the delicate man at the counter ducking into a crouch and crawling past the bleeding clerk to huddle with his family on the floor.

Pete walked toward the gunman, inviting a bullet.

"Either give me the gun or pull the trigger, son. Your choice."

The gunman held the gun with frozen arms and backed away from Pete.

"GET ON THE FLOOR, BITCH!!!"

Pete looked down at the fallen clerk and shook his head in disgust.

"I think you're the one who's going to be on the floor, kid."

I barked my head off in the van as the stinky gunman's two stinky friends left their posts at the sliding glass doors. Pulling semi-automatic pistols out of their loose clothing, they began walking toward Register 4, triangulating on Pete. Three guns to zero.

"You boys think you're good enough to hit my heart with all three bullets at the exact same time?"

Pete stood with his hands at his sides as the family held their breath. Silence flooded the supermarket as three stinky fingers shivered on sweaty triggers. I heard nothing but heartbeats and the humming buzz of overhead fluorescent lighting for five seconds. A surveillance monitor on the ceiling captured the holdup scene, but Pete was not in the footage.

"Give it a shot," Pete said. "On the count of three. One... two..."

"Am I interrupting something here, brother?"

Mag broke the silence, emerging from the produce section, marching through Register 7 to the front of the store like an unapologetic latecomer to a party. He looked at Pete, the family, and the three gunmen.

"I see you found the batteries --"

POP POP POP POP -- POP -- POP -- POP POP
POP -- POP -- POP --

Open fire. Weapons emptied into Mag, the sound of gunfire turning to empty metallic clicks as bullets thudded into Mag's thick body. Hot lead rounds fell to the cold floor, scattering like bouncing jellybeans at Mag's feet. The two stinky friends turned as if they'd seen a bear, fleeing out the doors to the parking lot. Mag sprinted after them.

The man and woman huddled over the child's choked screams as the first stinky gunman stood stiff, still holding his weapon on Pete.

"Still got a round in that thing?" Pete stared down the barrel. "Looks like your homeboys left you stranded."

Pete grabbed the stinky gunman by the wrist and spun him around, the empty gun falling to the floor. The stinky man yelped as Pete snapped his elbow, folding the stinky right arm backwards. With the back of the stinky right hand flat against the stinky right shoulder blade, Pete grabbed the stinky left hand, crushing the stinky fingers like a soft-boiled egg in his grip. The stinky man fell to the floor in shrieks.

"You won't be hitting anybody for a while."

Pete kicked the gun away and stood over the writhing stinky man. Lifting up his combat boot, he drove his heel into his stinky knee.

SNAP.

The stinky man squealed in agony. "WHAT TH --"

"Just so I know you're not going to run off --"

Pete repeated with the other leg, driving his thick-soled heel into the floor, snapping the other stinky knee. *SNAP.* The stinky man's screams went up an octave as he writhed on the floor like an abandoned germ. Unable to stand, unable to crawl.

"Now..."

Pete put his combat boot on the stinky man's neck and looked at the family.

"What's your boy's name, sir?"

"Yoshi."

Pete pressed his boot into the stinky man's neck.

"Apologize to Yoshi."

The stinky man growled, his cheek flat against the floor, trying to compose words with his stinky tongue.

"Apologize to Yoshi, or I'll snap your head off."

"SORRY!!! I'M SORRY!!! I'M --"

"Say 'I'm sorry, Yoshi.'"

"I'M SORRY YOSHI!!! I'M SORRY YOSHI!!!"

"'I'm a very bad man, Yoshi. Very bad.'"

"I'M A VERY BAD MAN YOSHI!!! I'M VERY BAD --"

"'And I'm going to pay for what I've done.'"

"I'M GOING TO PAY YOSHI!!! I'M GOING TO PAY FOR WHAT I'VE DONE YOSHI!!!"

Pete lifted his boot off the stinky man's neck and walked to the fallen clerk, lying in her own blood. He dropped to his knee and checked for a pulse. Nothing.

"Do you know her?"

Pete looked across the floor past the squirming maggot to the family against the front wall.

"No," the father said. "We were just picking up a prescription."

Pete stood up.

"And you saw the whole thing?"

The father nodded.

"The three came in, and then this man told her to give him the cash. She just laughed. Must have thought he was joking. This man shot her without warning. No warning."

Pete walked to the family and took a knee. The mother, hurt but conscious, sat against the wall of batteries, mouth bleeding, consoling her moaning child. Pete took off his trench coat and placed it on the boy, then strode over to a freezer unit near the door and fetched a bag of cocktail ice.

"I'm sorry this happened," Pete said, handing the ice to the woman. "Just remember --"

Mag ran back into the supermarket from the parking lot.

"Everybody okay, brother?"

Mag looked down at the dead woman behind the counter and winced, turning back to look down at the stinky man.

"Your buddies won't be coming back for you, brother. Looks like you'll need to bum a ride in a black and white."

Pete crouched near the family and grabbed a handful of batteries from the front wall, stuffing the plastic and cardboard packages into his vest pockets. He spoke in a new state of calm.

"You'll never forget what you saw tonight, Yoshi."

Pete put his palm on the young boy's head.

"But that's okay. Because when you do think of this night, you'll remember how it made you stronger."

Pete got to his feet and walked to the squirming maggot, nudging it with his boot. He turned back to the man and woman.

"This guy won't be going anywhere. Do you have a cell phone?"

"Yes," the father said.

"Call nine-one-one. The police will be here soon. Tell them everything you saw."

"But…"

Pete pointed to the ceiling. "And they have the video."

"But," the father repeated, pointing to Mag. "They shot your friend. How did he…"

Pete secured the buckles of his vest pockets as Mag walked out to the parking lot.

"We have to go now. There are others in the back freezer. Call nine-one-one."

Pete slapped a twenty-dollar bill on the counter of Register 4 as the father pulled out his cell phone and dialed. The mother wrapped up the petrified boy in Pete's trench coat and cradled him in her arms.

"Remember what I told you, Yoshi…"

Pete walked to the family and squatted down one last time.

"You remember what I told you, yes? What did I tell you?"

The boy stared at Pete in the eyes, captivated. Nodding his little head, he finally spoke.

"Stronger."

CHAPTER EIGHT

KABOOM!!! February 25, 1942, 03:14 AM. Our kitchen windows shook in the dark as anti-aircraft guns shot 12.8-pound rounds into the winter sky, blackout sirens blaring throughout the city. I wasn't even an hour old, and Los Angeles was already being attacked.

KABOOM!!! KABOOM!!! KABOOM!!!

Pete bolted back through the front door with his unlit flashlight, leaving our neighbors outside in their pajamas to shout amongst themselves above the sirens. Panic and confusion ran through the dark streets of Los Angeles as residents pointed to a chilled sky flooded with searchlights.

"They're coming in from the sky, Bea."

"What's going on?" Bea said. "Are we getting attacked?"

"Keep the lights off."

Wearing a trench coat, Pete took a knee next to us in the kitchen lit only by candles.

"How's she doing now?"

Beatrice, attractive and capable, sat flat on the floor in her bathrobe, tending to the thirteen of us and our mother. The smell of cooked tomatoes and garlic lingered in the kitchen from the night before.

"Her breathing is getting slow."

Pete held his palm to my mother's belly. She had been sick for weeks.

"How many?"

KABOOM!!! KABOOM!!! KABOOM!!!

Pete turned his flashlight on and shined it on me and my family.

"Thirteen," Beatrice said, picking me up and wrapping me in a clean dishtowel. "All stillborn except this one. He's a kicker."

Pete took me from Beatrice's hands and held me like a wrapped potato, shining his flashlight in my face.

"Shadow," Pete said for the first time. "Born into darkness. Hey there, little soldier --"

KABOOM!!! KABOOM!!! KABOOM!!!

I come from good roots. They gave us each just one name: Dash, Kona, Ace, Jackson. Ghost. My ancestors and friends are among the hundreds of four-legged soldiers to be trained here, and the first to be killed in the line of duty for the United States. Throughout the decades, dozens of us have been buried here at the K-9 Command Cemetery behind the fort's chapel.

KABOOM!!! KABOOM!!! KABOOM!!!

It had been just weeks since the attack on our cousins at Pearl Harbor in the Pacific, and our city was on full alert. Enemy air raids on the west coast of the United States had become a real possibility, with the Los Angeles Harbor being a particularly tempting target for any enemy wishing to cripple our nation. In the weeks following Pearl Harbor and leading up to my birth, city officials conducted nightly blackouts to eliminate any potential ground targets for an airborne enemy. Not a plugged light in the city remained on during these blackouts. Not even an automobile headlight.

KABOOM!!! KABOOM!!! KABOOM!!!

Pete put me down against my mother and took a seat at the dining table, his silhouette splashing across the flat ceiling. He picked up his black rotary telephone and dialed, pressing the receiver against his ear. It was a special line that only Pete used, installed next to our main telephone.

"It's Durante. We counted twenty-five silver objects."

KABOOM!!! KABOOM!!! KABOOM!!!

Pete plugged his other ear with his finger and leaned forward with his elbows on the table, listening.

"Not balloons. And too slow to be aircraft --"

KABOOM!!! KABOOM!!! KABOOM!!! Another wave of relentless explosions began.

"Hundreds of thousands of witnesses?" Pete shouted into the phone.

KABOOM!!! KABOOM!!! KABOOM!!!

"Has anything been hit?"

KABOOM!!! KABOOM!!! KABOOM!!!

"How do we know it's not something else?"

KABOOM!!! KABOOM!!! KABOOM!!!

Beatrice sat with us on the floor of the tight kitchen, wiping off my brothers and sisters with towels as I wriggled against the belly of my mother. Her heartbeat couldn't find a groove, constantly interrupted by the percussive thumps of our fort's cannons less than a mile away.

"I'll be there in ten minutes."

KABOOM!!! KABOOM!!! KABOOM!!!

Pete hung up the phone and got off his chair, crouching down next to us with his flashlight.

"Is it real this time?" Beatrice asked.

"Don't know yet. It started in Santa Monica. Now Naylor says they just saw a V formation over Long Beach. They're not from here."

"You mean --"

KABOOM!!! KABOOM!!! KABOOM!!!

"Unidentified."

"Dear Lord..."

KABOOM!!! KABOOM!!! KABOOM!!!

Pete got on his knees and knelt over my mother, taking her head in his hands. He held his face against hers, breathing deeply through his nose, inhaling the smell of her into his lungs.

"Ghostie, girl --"

KABOOM!!! KABOOM!!! KABOOM!!!

Pete sat up and pecked Beatrice on the cheek. He grabbed his flashlight and got to his feet.

"I have to go down there. Stay inside. Lights out."

KABOOM!!! KABOOM!!! KABOOM!!!

Pete pulled a revolver from his coat pocket and checked the chambers. With a backhanded flick of the wrist, he jerked the weapon shut with a hard metallic clack and placed it on the table.

"Keep her comfortable and make sure she feeds the pup," Pete continued. "First two days are critical."

"Got it."

"Gun's loaded."

"Got it."

"I love you."

"I love you."

Pete rushed back out into the explosive night with his flashlight, slamming the front door behind him.

KABOOM!!! KABOOM!!! KABOOM!!!

Beatrice stroked my mother's ears, her whispers smoothing off the harsh edges from the explosions outside.

"Hang in there, baby."

Beatrice wedged me into the crook of my mother's warmth, gently gathering my siblings and setting them on a thick towel on the floor near us.

"Your brother's going to make it for all of you. Shadow the Strong."

KABOOM!!! KABOOM!!! KABOOM!!!

Beatrice got to her feet and left the candlelit kitchen, walking through our dark house by memory. She went to the bedroom and grabbed the ticking clock from the nightstand.

KABOOM!!! KABOOM!!! KABOOM!!!

Beatrice returned to the kitchen with the ticking clock.

"We'll get you used to this, boy. It'll be almost as good as your mama."

Beatrice wound the clock and set it next to me, its consistent ticks mixing with my mother's slowing heartbeat. She caressed my mother's face.

"I'll be right back, baby. I need to get a box out in the garage."

KABOOM!!! KABOOM!!! KABOOM!!!

Beatrice disappeared out the kitchen door while I suckled for my first taste of milk, my mother's labored breathing continuing to slow. Her furry chest moaned as two defined arms with thick leathery hands reached down from the darkness, grabbing my brothers and sisters one by one, placing them in a bucket like an orchard farmer gathering fallen apples. I would see those two arms again. A dirty cast on the left, a tattoo of two black wings on the right.

KABOOM!!! KABOOM!!! KABOOM!!!

CHAPTER NINE

LEGS STRETCHED OUT with his crusty boots on the van's dashboard, Pete sat shotgun. I propped myself up next to his boots and looked out the windshield. Mag drove us out of the deserted supermarket parking lot with the headlights off, blues music bleeding through the radio's speaker.

"You know what the first rule of singing the blues is. Right, brother?"

"What's that?"

"Don't matter the song," Mag explained. "You always gotta start off with the part about you woke up this morning. Otherwise the song don't make no sense, you know? If you're sleeping, you got no song."

Mag sung the cliché lyric that we've heard a million times, grunting it out like a bluesy pro. *"I woke up this morning…"*

Pete eyed me. Studying.

"Make a left at the light. We'll cut through."

Distant sirens got louder as we coasted down the hill overlooking the harbor, streetlights passing us overhead like hypnotic shooting stars. Mag hung a quick left off the main street and into a neighborhood, away from the traffic lights and out of the path of any oncoming dispatch.

"Where to?"

"Harold's." Pete stared at me. "We need to stop at Harold's Place."

Mag scratched my head.

"My boy El Briga works the door of that joint. You been there?"

"I used to know the owner. Make a right on Twenty-second."

Mag hung a sharp right at the corner, taking us down a dark and narrow residential street crowded with parked cars. Pete looked out the dark window, rapping his knuckles against the smudged glass.

"I can use a drink anyway."

Mag pulled the van up to the red curb in front of a loud dive bar on Pacific Avenue, the main drag through the seedier part of town. A whirlpool of comers and goers spilled in and out of the bar while a burly tattooed bouncer, probably more drunk than the patrons, loosely checked identification. A scrappy mutt sat at his feet on the sidewalk.

Mag stepped out to the street and shut the door, walking around the front of the van toward the crowd. He held up his broad arms and shouted above the music coming from inside.

"What's up, brother!"

"Perrier!" The bouncer had the growl of a bulldog. "Hey, bro!"

The two collided in a chest-bumping embrace.

Pete dropped his feet from the dashboard and sat up, opening the van door, turning to scratch my chin as I stood up to scan the perimeter around the van through the dirty windows. A lonely figure with nowhere to go wandered along the sidewalk across the street, pushing a shopping cart full of useless belongings, having a discussion with somebody I couldn't see. Mag stood at the door of the bar talking to the bouncer in the middle of the small swarming crowd.

"Stay here, little soldier. We'll be right back."

Pete stepped out to the curb and threw the van door shut, walking across the sidewalk to the bar's entrance. He took a knee next to the scrappy mutt at Mag's feet, letting her smell me on his hand. She sat up and licked his knuckles.

"Hey, gorgeous."

"That'd be Gloria," said Mag. "She's on my schedule next month. And this is my man El Briga. We go way back."

"At least," the bouncer said, his filthy grin reeking of alcohol and cigarette tar.

"This is my boy Pete," Mag continued. "Pete's got some unfinished business we're taking care of tonight."

El Briga grabbed Pete's arm and pulled him close for a quick obligatory bear hug.

"Perrier only picks the best ones, bro --"

"I'll catch you on the way out, brother." Mag knocked fists with El Briga and disappeared through the bar's entrance.

Pete began to follow.

"Pete," El Briga blurted. "Peter Durante?"

Pete stopped in the doorway and turned.

"That's right."

El Briga reached into his back pocket and pulled out a folded white envelope.

"Somebody left this for you, bro."

"Who? When?"

"Can't say, bro."

"Thanks," Pete said. *Greamer.*

Pete took the folded envelope and entered the stuffy bar, wincing at the blaring deejay music that could only be described as a mashed-up reggae hip-hop electronic nightmare. Christmas lights lined walls covered with illuminated beer signs; red, white, and blue ribbons from a forgotten Fourth of July still dangled from ceiling fans that didn't work. Three tattered pool tables sat like islands as bored minglers danced for an imaginary audience.

Pete unfolded the sealed envelope in his hand. Branded into the envelope, inkless:

PETER DURANTE

Pete opened the envelope's seal and pulled out a crisp white note. Walking to one of the pool tables, he unfolded the note and held it under the bright fluorescent light. On it were seven words:

- - - - -

When the flower shakes: *HERO HITS WEDGE*

- - - - -

"Whatcha got there, brother?"

"*When the flower shakes, hero hits wedge.*" Pete looked across the pool table at Mag. "Greamer left me another key."

"What is it?"

"Not sure yet. I need a couple shots of something."

Pete and Mag walked from the pool table to the end of the bar and claimed two empty stools. Mag winked at the woman behind the bar and held up six fingers as Pete sat down.

"Your buddy at the door," Pete said. "Called you Perrier --"

"My last name."

Pete placed the note on the bar in front of him and stared at the room through the mirror behind the liquor bottles on the back shelf. He glanced at a neon clock on the far wall behind him, flipping its image horizontally in his mind. Leaning forward with his elbows on the sticky bar top, he pushed his fingernails into his scalp and began studying the note.

When the flower shakes. Hero hits wedge. Flower?

"Stumped?" Mag asked.

The bartender lined up six shot glasses, filling them with a rich amber liquid.

"Thank you, darlin'." Mag grabbed two of the glasses, handing one to Pete. "Cheers, brother. To heroes, flowers, and wedges. And finding the *Triad of Hell*."

The two clinked glasses, swallowing the liquid. Pete slammed the glass down and grabbed a second, throwing it down his throat. He slammed the glass down and grabbed a third full glass, holding it up to propose a toast of his own.

"Drinkin' like a man in a hurry to die," Mag said, grabbing his second glass. "I'll drink to that."

"To getting my family back."

Pete tilted his head back and shot the booze, slamming the glass down on the bar as he stood from the stool and grabbed the note.

"I need to think about this for a minute. Alone. Then we need to split."

Pete walked from the bar to the far end of the room, finding a corner with an empty shuffleboard table and the fermenting smell of old carpet splashed with cuspy pineapple juice. He leaned against the wall and read the note:

\- - - - -

When the flower shakes: HERO HITS WEDGE

\- - - - -

"Shit."

Pete reached into his chest pocket and pulled out Greamer's key from the diner. He unfolded it and read it again:

\- - - - -

Read Instructions. Enigma.

Just

Know

Man

Never

Reverses

His

Choice.

Resolve,

His

Journey's

Key.

\- - - - -

Pete paced in the corner, comparing the two notes side by side in his hands.

"Are you going to war?"

Pete looked up, stunned. A girl, probably too pretty to be in such a place, was sizing him up from head to toe. Tall and slim, she had long tendrils of black seaweed-like hair that cascaded over her pasty bare shoulders to match her dress. She was clearly forward, and not the least bit shy, yet somehow a picture of innocence.

"What?"

"Your pants," she said.

Pete looked down at his fatigues and combat boots.

"Oh, yeah, war. You can say that."

"I'm digging your style," she said. "You live around here?"

"You can say that." Pete found her words both contrived and oddly endearing.

"I've never seen you here before."

"I used to know the owner," Pete said, folding the two notes and shoving them into a vest pocket. "Haven't gotten out much. I'm way too old for you, sweetheart."

The girl laughed.

"Too old? What are you, thirty?"

"You can say that."

"What were you reading?"

"Nothing."

"What's your name?"

This one won't be giving up soon. Pete shook his head and granted her a friendly smile for her efforts. "What's yours?"

"Guess." The girl grinned, fondling her hoop earring, finding the sexual tension she craved.

"Mary?"

She shook her head.

"Then it must be Zeke."

"Ha ha. No."

"Cleopatra?"

"I'll give you a hint. It's a flower."

Pete touched his vest pocket, staring into her dark brown eyes with a new interest. *When the flower shakes.*

"A flower, eh? How about Daisy."

She shook her head.

"Lily?"

"Nope."

Could it be Violet? Like PURPLE? Pete's mind spun in silence, trying to find relevance in anything.

"Is it Violet?"

And then it hit. I barked as the van tilted back and forth, bouncing up and down on the pavement at the curb.

"EARTHQUAKE!!! EARTHQUAKE!!!"

People in the bar screamed as the entire building shifted back and forth in violent jolts. Billiard balls knocked dirty felt tabletops as the ground rumbled underfoot, lamps and broken fans swinging from the ceiling. Liquor bottles fell from the shelves behind the bar as people braced themselves against the walls and ducked for cover. The girl's startled body jerked as she fell into Pete's arms.

"EARTHQUAKE!!!"

The world's adrenaline rattled for what seemed like minutes, eventually tapering off into a gentle sway. Pete helped the girl to her feet as people laughed amongst themselves, giving each other high fives as the deejay's music resumed. Just another night in Los Angeles.

"What's your name?" Pete asked. "Tell me your name."

The girl smiled, exhilarated, shocked. She straightened her dress out at the knees.

"It's Rosalinda."

Rosalinda. Rose. When the flower shakes. "*Hero hits wedge,*" Pete muttered.

"What?" she asked.

"What's your last name?"

She smiled.

"Guess. It starts with an *O.*"

Pete groaned, in no mood for more games. *Hero hits wedge. Hero hits wedge...*

"*O* can't work," he mumbled.

"Can't work for what?"

Pete pulled out the note from his vest pocket and studied it again.

– – – – –

When the flower shakes: HERO HITS WEDGE

– – – – –

Hero hits wedge. Edge. Greed. Heist... "Son of a..."

Pete turned from the girl and darted through the mess of partiers, finding Mag sitting at the bar.

"What's shaking, brother?" Mag laughed.

"We need to go. Now."

Pete flattened the note out on the wet bar for Mag.

— — — — —

When the flower shakes: HERO HITS WEDGE

— — — — —

Pete slapped his palm on the note, scrunching it into a ball in his hand.

"*Hero hits wedge*! *WHERE IS THE DOG*???"

CHAPTER TEN

Over there, over there,
Send the word, send the word over there
That the Yanks are coming, the Yanks are coming,
The drums rum-tumming everywhere.
So prepare, say a prayer,
Send the word, send the word to beware,
We'll be over, we're coming over,
And we won't come back till it's over over there.

And like the song goes, it was finally over over there. For most of us, anyway.

The sun was setting on one of the most significant days in history. Our house smelled like freshly baked garlic bread, Beatrice was draining the pasta, and I sat in my favorite place under the dining table as we listened to the news on the radio. Pete would be home any minute.

A man's voice blared through our kitchen radio's speaker.

"With the formal Japanese surrender taking place on board the battleship U.S.S. Missouri in Tokyo Bay earlier today, President Truman has declared this day, September Second, to be V-J Day. Victory over Japan..."

It was late summer of 1945, two years after we lost Dad. With the German forces surrendering in Europe that spring, we'd spent our entire summer contemplating how we would force Japan and its stubborn leaders to throw in the towel as well. The Imperial Japanese Navy had ceased to exist, and an Allied invasion of Japan was imminent. By summertime, it was in order for us to put one last bullet in the Axis powers and call it a day.

Pete walked through the front door, exhausted and smelling of champagne. He sat down on our brand new couch and unlaced his boots.

"One hell of a party out there, Bea! Streets are crazy!"

"We heard. Thank goodness." Beatrice dried her hands on her apron and reached across the counter to turn the radio off. On her ring finger was the gold band with engraved letters: *DREAM TURNS*.

Pete got up in his socks and walked across the new wood floor to the kitchen, washing his hands in the sink. Splashing water onto his face and drying it with a dishtowel hanging from the oven, he grabbed a glass from the cupboard and filled it with cold water.

"Big shindig down at the Red. Smells good in here --"

Pete welcomed Beatrice's lips to his.

"Sit down and I'll fix you a plate."

Things had come to a head a few weeks earlier. After Japanese officials ignored multiple warnings to surrender, our president made the decision to rapidly and decisively obliterate every productive enterprise they had above ground. From their docks, to their factories, to their communications, we vowed to completely destroy Japan's power to make war. On August 6 and 9, as threatened, we dropped atomic bombs on Hiroshima and Nagasaki, respectively.

This move has been a source of scholarly debate ever since. Opposition calls the decision fundamentally immoral, racist, and dehumanizing, while supporters see the bombings as the necessary means to an end, ultimately saving lives that would've been lost in an invasion, and quite simply the result of Japanese leaders refusing to surrender when they had the chance. All opinions aside, the dropping of these bombs put an end to the war once and for all. With Japan finally surrendering in August, World War II had officially come to a close.

Pete sat down to a plate full of steaming pasta and meatballs, exhaling a sigh of relief that he'd been holding in for years. He rubbed my head with his socked feet.

"Hey there, little soldier. They finally cried uncle. They signed on the line."

Beatrice sat down at the other end of the table, holding a pad of paper covered with her handwriting. Beaming, she placed the notepad in front of her.

"It's over, Bea. I told Naylor I quit."

"What did he say?"

"He's happy for us."

Pete spun his fork in the marinara-drenched spaghetti, lanced a meatball, and shoved it in his mouth.

"I told him I want nothing to do with crypto anymore now that the war's over. No more decoding, no more puzzles, no more breaking my brain over cryptic messages. Leaving it all behind. I'm a civilian now. Told him I'm going into woodworking full time."

Pete was an excellent craftsman.

"We'll settle down like we always talked about. No more secrets. I just got an order for another set of chairs from the guys at the club."

Beatrice smiled, holding up her glass of water. "To new beginnings."

Pete wiped his lips with his napkin and swallowed, grabbing his glass and holding it out to hers. "New beginnings, love. I like that."

"I have something for you." Beatrice put down her glass and tore a page from her notepad, sliding it across the dining table. "It took me hours!"

Pete put down his glass and picked up the piece of paper. On it were two words in her handwriting:

UNTITLED ALERT

"How in Heaven do you do this stuff?" Beatrice put her elbows on the table. "It's so neat. I don't know how you do it."

Pete stared at the note and arched his eyebrows, nodding like an impressed coach.

"You did this by yourself?"

Beatrice nodded with a proud grin.

Pete glued his eyes to the paper and rearranged the characters in his mind.

UNTITLED ALERT

Beatrice sat at the edge of her seat, watching Pete think.

"Wait --" Pete put the note down with a nervous smile. "Are you kidding me? You're serious?"

Beatrice smiled and nodded her head *yes*.

"Yes? You're kidding."

"No," Beatrice said. "I'm not kidding. Yes. I'm serious."

"Seriously?"

"Seriously."

Pete tilted his head and smiled, looking down at the note, marveling at the two words.

"When?"

"Spring. I found out this morning."

Pete stood from his chair and walked to the other end of the table. He tucked a loose strand of Beatrice's hair behind her ear and kissed her lips.

"God, look what I've done to you. Well done, doll. You're a natural."

Beatrice laughed.

"I have a good teacher."

Pete looked at the ceiling and scrunched his eyebrows.

"Wait, you're serious?"

"I'm serious."

Pete's face froze with a reluctant smile.

"You're not kidding?"

"I'm serious." Beatrice grinned. "And I'm not kidding."

"Oh my God, it's a miracle!" Pete crouched over Beatrice at the table, rubbing her belly. "Wait! This calls for more champagne --"

RIIINNNG. RIIINNNG --

"Shit," Pete said. "Hold that thought --"

Pete leaned over and grabbed his special black telephone from the table.

RIIINNNG --

"Happy First Annual V-J Day, Durante speaking."

Pete turned and winked at us, holding the handset to his ear.

"Yes."

Pete's smile disappeared. He looked at Beatrice and wrinkled his brow.

"Now? Can't it wait?"

Pete held the phone over his eyes.

"A key distribution? For what? Who is he?"

"What is it?" Beatrice asked.

Pete shook his head and mouthed the postponing words. *Quiet for a second.* He spoke back into the phone.

"Is he Black Chamber?"

Pete leaned against the wall. Rain on the parade.

"I just saw Andreas at the Red. I don't know where Carroll is."

Pete looked at the ceiling and closed his eyes.

"Who else knows about this? Have you talked to Sal?" Pete paced back and forth, chained to the wall by the telephone cord. "Aw, shit --"

Beatrice reached down and rubbed my ears.

"Yeah," Pete said. "Yes, of course. I'll be right there."

Pete placed the handset on the hook and slammed the phone back on the table.

"What is it?" Beatrice asked.

Pete turned and planted his palms flat on the dining table, shifting his weight to his hands, staring at the floor through his dinner.

"That was Naylor down at H.Q. Somebody's called a key distribution meeting. It's mandatory. I have to go."

"Didn't you tell him you quit?"

Pete stood up straight.

"It's probably just a debriefing," Pete said. "There's a special agent there for a transfer of intel. Shouldn't take too long."

Pete took Beatrice's face in his hands and kissed her forehead.

"It's a miracle, Bea!"

Beatrice stood from the table.

"You haven't eaten --"

"Keep it warm for me."

Pete took a knee and made eye contact with me under the table.

"And you. We'll go toss the ball around when I get back. Deal?"

Deal.

Pete walked to the couch and sat down, shoving his sweaty feet back into his boots.

"I'll be back as soon as I can. Or I'll call."

"Here, take something to go."

Beatrice scrambled in the kitchen to grab a bowl from the cupboard and a roll of tin foil from a drawer. She took Pete's plate from the table and scraped the pasta and meatballs into the bowl, topped it off with two pieces of bread, and sealed it all with foil. Grabbing a fork, she walked into the living room as Pete stood up from the couch in his boots. She handed him the wrapped meal.

"Thanks, love." Pete took the food and grabbed his keys. "I'll call you later."

Pete opened the front door and stopped on the threshold.

"*Untitled alert*. You're good."

He smiled.

"I'm not done with you, woman. We have lots of celebrating to do when I get back."

Beatrice laughed and kissed Pete, closing the front door behind him as she'd done many times. She turned and walked back into the kitchen, taking a sip from his glass.

"Looks like it's just us tonight again, Shadow. Just the three of us."

Beatrice sat down and flipped through the first few folded pages of her notepad, each covered with her scribbles and various combinations of letters and phrases. The jotted aftermath of an afternoon spent creating the playfully cryptic message for Pete, getting into his world. She reviewed her work with a smile.

At the bottom of the last page, circled, her chosen final message:

UNTITLED ALERT

She flipped backward through pages of the notepad, reading the words that systematically led up to her circled masterpiece.

DETAIL...

TIRADE...

ALLURED...

RATTLED...

RELATED...

TURNED...

Beatrice flipped over to the front page of the notepad and smiled at what she'd written at the top earlier that afternoon. The two words that served as the starting point for her cryptic exercise.

LITTLE DURANTE

CHAPTER ELEVEN

Mag's van waited at the curb outside Harold's Place, its windows shattered. Pete ran out from the bar and called for me between whistles.

"Shadow!.. Shadow!... Shadow!..."

Half a block away, a pickup truck was stopped in the middle of the street, door open, idling. The driver stood on the street, distraught, looking down at me. I lay motionless on the headlight-flooded asphalt several feet in front of the truck.

"SHADOW!!!"

Pete bolted over to me and dropped to his knees. He listened for a heartbeat.

"LITTLE SOLDIER!!! NO!!!"

"I didn't see him," the driver moaned, babbling in dumb shock. "He just ran in front of me... I didn't see him..."

Pete sprang to his feet.

"YOU FUCKING IDIOT!!!"

Pete lunged for the driver's throat with both hands, going in for the kill before instinctively pulling back and turning away. He paced the street, hands on his head, anger turning to despair. He cursed at the sky like a man mad at God. A small crowd gathered at the curb.

"FUCK!!! GODDAMN FUCK!!!"

Mag's calm voice plodded through Pete's screams.

"Lucky Thirteen..."

"FUCK!!! I CAN'T SAVE HER WITHOUT THE DOG!!!"

Mag trotted from the curb to the middle of the street and crouched over me, whispering.

"Lucky Thirteen..."

Mag reached his thick leathery hand down to my neck and checked for a pulse. Pete stopped screaming as the handful of onlookers began spilling into the street.

"Lucky Thirteen --"

I bounced to my feet like a spring. Full of life. No open wounds, but hey, you'd probably get the wind knocked out of you too if you got hit by a truck. I padded over to Pete.

"Now let's find that book, Lucky Thirteen!" Mag laughed. "You ready to find that book for Uncle Rip?"

Pete dropped to a knee and embraced me. Relieved.

"What did you do, Perrier?"

"You should know by now I got a way with dogs, brother. Now let's go. Sunrise'll be here soon."

Mag kept his distance, eyeing us like a hawk. Pete whispered into my ear.

"This is it, little soldier. I'm putting all my trust in you now. Lead the way. Find the *Triad of Hell*. Take us to our girls --"

"Sunrise, brother." Mag had grown impatient. "Quota. Rip'll sling my ass if I don't make quota."

"Yeah, yeah, yeah," Pete said. "We're coming. Get the bags from the van."

Pete got to his feet and continued, staring me in the eyes.

"I need you to take us to our girls. You got a problem with that?"

Nope.

"Of course you don't. You're my little soldier."

Pete and Mag carried our rucksacks of gear as I led us on a leashless two-mile hump from Harold's. Cutting through sleepy side streets and dark alleyways, I stopped at a tall chain link fence that surrounded Fort MacArthur, a historic military installation that was no longer in operation. The place had the stillness and heavy silence of a graveyard.

"This is it, Perrier," Pete said.

Pete hurled his rucksack over the rusty barbed wire strands strung along the top edge of the fence. It landed in the brush with the deadened clatter of a pillowcase full of spoons.

"Where to, little soldier?"

Pete walked me down to the corner and pulled back on a small inconspicuous portion of the fence that he'd cut years before, holding it open as I squeezed through. He followed.

"Let's go, Perrier."

Tossing his rucksack over the fence, Mag stuck his thick fingers through the chain links and pulled himself up like a heavy gymnast, heaving his body over the corroded barbed wire and into the brush. He picked up his rucksack.

"How big is this place, brother?"

Pete pulled out a flashlight and flipped the switch, swinging his rucksack over his shoulder.

"Big enough. What kind of name is Perrier, anyway? French?"

CHAPTER TWELVE

NOBODY BUT THE THREE OF US and the drone of a foghorn. I took point, marching us through the same dark fields we'd explored many, many times in the daylight. The brush began getting thicker as we hiked, with overgrown weeds taller than the tops of my ears. I knew the area like the back of my paw.

"He's taking us under the battery," Pete said. "To the meeting room."

Humping through the brushy gopher-infested fields overlooking our fort's chapel and K-9 Command Cemetery, we reached a clearing at the top edge of Battery Barlow-Saxton, a concrete firing pit the size of a football field and about thirty feet deep. Barred openings and steel doors lined the pit's concrete walls beneath layers of graffiti, with bridges and stairways descending down to the concrete floor.

"What was this place for, brother?"

Mag stood at the steep edge of the pit's urban ruins, his bloodshot eyes adjusting in the moonlight.

"Kicking ass," Pete said, trailing me down the concrete steps. "*Follow the dog.*"

During the war years, the United States Army could use the firing pit to defend an attack on the shores of Los Angeles from any angle. Arced rounds could be blasted into the sky, hitting battleships with downward mortar fire. If our guys got the math right, they could sink an enemy ship eleven miles offshore.

"Another text..."

Pete stopped halfway down the concrete steps and pulled his cell phone from his pocket, reading the glowing display.

"From Rip again?" Mag hurried down the concrete steps behind Pete. "What's it say?"

"*Don't stop to smell the roses.*" Pete shoved his phone back into his pocket.

Pete followed me down the concrete steps and into the pit. Reaching the floor, I scouted out the edges and corners of the hard perimeter and took a quick inventory with my nose. Nothing unusual.

"Over here," Pete said.

Mag followed us across the pit to a barred iron gate in front of a doorway leading into the thick concrete wall. Pete forced his way through the loose gate, its hinges already broken.

"Get your light out."

I led our flashlight beams through the broken gate and down a tight concrete stairway descending beneath the battery. Rusted doors lined the passage, welded shut, corroded from lifetimes of dank ocean air. Metal piping ran across the low-hanging flaked concrete ceiling of the chilled concrete stairwell.

The cascading narrow passage opened into a cold hard room, its floor littered with dust-covered office papers. Boxes remained stacked on shelves against one wall, with desks and chairs still sitting where they'd been abandoned many decades prior. The room was only one in a complex maze of offices connected by open doorways, with square glassless windows revealing adjacent rooms and halls separated by concrete walls.

Pete scanned the room with his flashlight. The whole place smelled like wet newspaper with traces of skunk.

Mag shined his flashlight to the top shelf on the wall. Square rotting tiles tried to unglue themselves from the ceiling, dripping with moisture and age. Mag set his light down and pulled boxes off the shelves, sifting through their contents. Medical supplies, bandages, even gas masks.

"Better find it fast, brother. Gotta have Lucky Thirteen in by sunrise."

Pete stood at the edge of the room, shining his flashlight through the doorway into a black void.

"Where to, little soldier?"

The guys followed me with their flashlights down a dark corridor and into a machinery room. Loose cut wires dangled from sheet metal boxes mounted on white enamel-covered brick walls. Conduits ran up from the floor and across the ceiling above a giant machine of valves, cylinders, and iron chambers. Buttons, switches, and levers painted red collected dust on steel cabinet doors.

"Take us, little soldier. Take us to the book."

I took us through the machine room and along a curved passage of the underground complex toward the smell of gunpowder, entering a hall filled with empty metal canisters and other debris. One wall was built from unpainted cinder blocks.

"Hold up!"

Mag shouted from the rear.

"Check this out, brother."

Mag stood shining his flashlight down into a gaping hole in the floor exposing a crawl space of twisted metal, cobwebs, and a dead cat. Cats are far less interesting when they're not moving.

"His tenth time down here?"

"*Follow the dog,*" Pete said, falling back to the rear.

Mag followed my tail as I zigzagged deeper through the halls and rooms of the complex, taking a shortcut through an old latrine. Washbasins with rotting hardware lined a mirrored wall. Pete stopped, shining his light in the mirror. Mag and I left the latrine, hanging a left under an arched doorway and down a long narrow corridor.

"Right behind you, Lucky Thirteen," Mag huffed. "Right behind you."

The smell was stronger than ever, but I could go no farther. Mag shouted.

"Lucky Thirteen found something."

Pete followed Mag's voice to find us at the end of a twisted passage blocked by a heavy steel door. It was either locked from behind or welded shut at the seams, with a sliding lever and latch that seemed to have melded into the door itself. Mag muscled the lever and kicked the door to no avail.

"Stuck, brother --"

"Stand back."

Pete pulled the lever. Nothing. He backed off and dropped his rucksack to the floor of filth, shining his light on the door.

"The Casimir effect," Pete said, tapping on the steel door with his flashlight. "Two doors spaced apart so the electromagnetic field's vacuum energy doesn't always obey the boundary conditions. Quantum field theory stuff. The dog can feel it."

Pete pulled on the lever. It didn't budge. He pulled on it again.

"You sure this is it, brother?"

Pete pulled on the lever again. Stuck.

"I'll be damned --"

Swinging his rucksack over his shoulder, Pete shouted with an angry urgency. His barking orders echoed through the underground complex.

"We need to go in from the other side. Out, little soldier, out! Now! Out! Out! Out..."

I turned and began retracing our steps through the gnarled complex, sniffing our way back to the entrance. Pete and Mag followed.

"Move it!"

CHAPTER THIRTEEN

PETE ENTERED the fort's upper reservation alone and walked across the dirt clearing to the top edge of Battery Barlow-Saxton, the concrete firing pit the size of a football field. Barred openings and steel doors lined the pit's clean concrete walls, with bridges and stairways descending down about thirty feet to the concrete floor.

"Sarge!"

A young guard in an Army Jeep skidded to a crunchy stop in the gravel, holding his right arm over a loose stack of canned beers in the passenger seat. Pete turned from the edge of the pit.

"It's over, Sarge! Truman called it! Wow, don't you look like a happy man!"

"All's right with the world, Smolensky. I just heard I'm going to be a father."

"How about that!" The young driver hooted with the enthusiasm a boy finds after a few beers. "Congratulations, Sarge! Hey, we're having our own celebration in the barracks if you want to double up with us. We can light up some cigars --"

"Not tonight," Pete said, smiling. "Maybe later."

"No canine today?"

"Not today."

"What'cha got there, Sarge?"

Pete looked down at Beatrice's foil-wrapped dinner in his hand and turned back toward the pit.

"Just some chow," Pete said. "I'll see you later, Smolensky. You ladies enjoy yourselves."

"Roger that!" The young driver slapped the stack of beers and popped the Jeep into gear, its tires spinning in the gravel as he sped away. "We'll keep some cold for you if you change your mind, old man! And congratulations again!"

Pete walked down the pit's steps and across its floor to a barred gate in front of a passage leading into the thick concrete wall. He pulled out his identification and showed it to a tall guard standing inside the gate.

"What's this all about?" Pete asked.

"Sergeant Peter Durante," the tall guard said, opening the gate. "Through there, sir. You're the last to arrive."

Pete descended the tight concrete stairwell under the battery toward the busy smell of coffee and cigarettes. Steel doors lined the lit passage, with metal piping running across the low-hanging concrete ceiling.

It's a girl.

Reaching the bottom of the underground passage, Pete stepped into a hard, stark office furnished with desks, chairs, shelves, and overhead lighting. It was only the first room in a complex maze of offices connected by open doorways, with square glassless windows revealing adjacent rooms and halls separated by concrete walls. People filled the room; some in uniform, clusters of others in street clothing.

"Two lines, please. Two lines..."

A busy uniformed officer instructed people where to stand.

"One line for men, another for women..."

"Hey, Pete, over here."

Fellow codebreaker Charlie stood in line chomping the last of an apple. The only face in the room Pete recognized. Always reeking of body odor, the scrawny 26-year-old had been cracking codes since college.

Before that, he had studied statistics in order to pursue a career in insurance. That was never to happen.

"Chuck," Pete said. "How long have you been here?"

"About twenty minutes."

"Who was the guy at the gate?" Pete asked, cutting in line behind Charlie. "Never saw him before."

An underground meeting room crowded with at least twenty people, both men and women, many of them with the scruffiness and eccentricities of overworked professors. Most of the men were unshaven, their fingernails stuffed with dirt, with clothing in a mass of creases. Pete and Charlie fit right in.

A lanky man wearing an ambiguous dark uniform stood at the front of the room, stirring black coffee with a knife.

Pete and Charlie moshed their way to the back wall and found John Andreas, a handsome tan-skinned man in his late thirties. The three men had all worked with a team of cryptanalysts a few years earlier to reverse-engineer an Enigma prototype.

"Ladies, gentlemen..."

The lanky man in dark began to speak, standing with his assistant at a large blackboard. A box of envelopes sat on a folding table in front of them.

"Thank you for coming on such short notice."

The man took inventory of the room's faces with his black eyes. He sipped his coffee, glaring at the back wall.

"Now that we're all here, I'll begin."

He spoke with a raspy deliberate voice.

"For thousands of years, kings, queens, and generals have relied on efficient and secret communication in order to govern their countries and command their armies. Codes and ciphers. Techniques for disguising messages."

The man smiled yellowness.

"This, of course, is nothing you're not familiar with. You are all among the best codebreakers history has ever seen..."

"Who is this guy, Johnny?" Pete whispered. "Black Chamber?"

Andreas shrugged his shoulders.

"Codebreakers like yourselves are linguistic alchemists," the lanky man in dark continued. "A mystical tribe conjuring sensible words out of meaningless symbols and gibberish."

The man handed his coffee to his assistant, picked up a piece of chalk, and turned to the blackboard. With scratching squeaks, he wrote large capital letters.

RIP GREAMER

"My name is Rip Greamer. Your superiors have graciously agreed to meet with me today. I've been a fan of your skills for a long time."

He turned and took a swig of coffee.

"I wanted to meet the best, and you're it."

He scoured the room of faces.

"A pack of hounds trying to pick up the scent. Geese that lay golden eggs and never cackle. The creative codebreaker must perforce commune daily with dark spirits to accomplish mental ju-jitsu. Your intellectual prowess is something I respect as much as do your leaders."

He spoke faster.

"Not only have you saved Allied and Russian lives, but you've saved German, Italian, and Japanese lives as well. This is the debt the world owes you. It is the crowning human value of your achievements. Heroes."

Greamer spoke with purpose, pointing his knife at faces in the room.

"The codebreaking craft is dominated by a bizarre combination of mathematicians, scientists, linguists, classicists, chess grandmasters, bridge experts, crossword puzzle addicts..."

Greamer pointed to a middle-aged woman in a floral-print shawl, sitting on a chair near the front wall.

"Joining us tonight is one of the world's best contract bridge players. Sunlighting as a homemaker."

Greamer laughed. The room nervously laughed with him, as if on cue.

"One of the free world's secret weapons. Like a wolf in the night, she does her damage unnoticed. Thank you for being here, ma'am."

Greamer pointed his knife at an old man in the front corner of the room.

"Also joining us tonight is a gentleman doing triple-duty. Not only is he a museum curator, he's also an authority on porcelain. Who would have known? Thank you for being here, sir."

Greamer's branchy arm pointed to the back wall.

"We even have an American elite with us tonight. A purebred Navajo. Would you please raise your hand, sir."

Andreas raised his hand and nodded with a stoic shyness. The room murmured with respect.

"The world owes you a great debt, sir," Greamer said. "There exists no purer concentration of Americanism than among the First Americans."

Greamer's eyes caught Pete's from across the crowded room.

"And standing next to Mr. Andreas, I understand we have a war dog trainer. Sergeant Peter Durante. Good evening to you, Sergeant."

Pete nodded. *How does he know me?*

"Intelligence." Greamer set his coffee on the table and turned to the blackboard, scratching a word in chalk:

INTELLIGENCE

"Nothing should be as favorably regarded as intelligence; nothing should be as generously rewarded as intelligence; nothing should be as confidential as the work of intelligence."

Greamer turned from the blackboard.

"And, as part of the Allied satellite cryptanalysis program, you have all agreed to keep your wartime efforts confidential. You are to speak to nobody of them. Not even amongst yourselves. I trust this is understood?"

The room mumbled affirmatively as Greamer took a long swig of coffee.

"I've spent some time with your British colleagues at Bletchley Park. Buckinghamshire, the home of the Government Code and Cipher School. As part of their Allied satellite program, you must be quite aware of their achievements. An exceptionally creative bunch they have there."

Greamer pulled the knife from his coffee, running his cadaverous tongue along its sharp edge.

"They're now busy on a new assignment, much like the one I need you for. Which, of course, brings us to the question you're all quietly asking yourselves."

Greamer threw up his arms and shouted.

"Why am I here? The war is over!"

Greamer dropped his arms and smiled, rolling his neck with a popping sound.

"I trust you will find your answer to that question in the months ahead. Thank you once again. Please cooperate with the guards on the way out."

CHAPTER FOURTEEN

"GENTLEMEN." A gruff guard in uniform tapped Charlie on the shoulder and pointed to Pete. "You two come with me."

Pete and Charlie followed the gruff guard out of the meeting room and down a corridor with surveillance cameras mounted on the ceiling. Neither man dared speak of the meeting, at least not in the presence of guards and cameras.

"My life's about to change, Chuck," Pete said.

Pete and Charlie followed the gruff guard, turning right twice and left once. Pete grinned from ear to ear.

"What's up?"

"The missus just gave me some big news. She's on the nest!"

Charlie dropped an apple core into his blazer pocket.

"Congratulations, buddy! Victory and stork. What a day for news!"

"And I'm quitting crypto once I un-enlist. Scaling down. Opening up my own woodworking business."

Charlie gave Pete a hearty slap on the back as they reached a long folding table next to a door leading to a room. Another guard sat behind the table, a surveillance camera mounted on the wall behind him.

"He'll take you from here," the gruff guard said. "Empty your pockets and leave your belongings on the table. Shirts and shoes as well. You'll get them back after the scan."

"Scan for what?" Charlie asked, tossing his corduroy blazer on the table and unbuttoning a disheveled flannel pajama shirt.

"Just protocol," said the table guard, holding out an index card. "You first, Mr. Carroll. Bring this with you through that door."

"Can I keep my glasses on?"

"Of course."

Charlie placed his shirt and loafers on the table and took the card from the officer.

"The hell is this?" Pete whispered.

"Your guess is as good as mine," Charlie mumbled. "I'll see you on the other side."

Charlie disappeared shirtless through the door with the index card as Pete unlaced his boots.

"Your pockets too, Sergeant."

"All this for a debriefing?" Pete asked, pulling his boots off. "Why the strip search?"

"It's for authentication is all, sir. Your tank top too, please."

The table guard handed Pete an index card. Printed on it:

PETER DURANTE

"Give this to the technician," the table guard said. "Then you can leave."

Pete placed his shirt, tank top, keys, wallet, and Beatrice's foil-wrapped pasta on the table and walked through the door.

A machinery room. Sheet metal boxes were mounted on white enamel-covered brick walls. Conduits ran up from the floor and across the ceiling above a giant machine of valves, cylinders, and iron chambers, with buttons, switches, and levers painted red on steel cabinet doors.

"Your card, sir."

A uniformed woman with stiff wavy hair took Pete's index card and fastened it to her clipboard. Pulling a thermometer from his mouth, she jotted down his weight as he stepped off the scale.

"Come with me, sir."

The uniformed woman escorted Pete to a small laboratory off the main machinery room. A male technician in a white lab coat sat on a stool in the corner beside something that looked like a dentist's chair, with wires and ten electrodes running from the chair to an electrocardiographic recorder. The device was equipped with buttons and an output mechanism of graph paper.

"Have a seat," the technician said. "Make yourself comfortable. This will only take a minute."

Everything was happening so fast. Pete took a seat in the chair, the vinyl cold against his bare skin.

"What is this?" Pete asked.

"We're authenticating your vitals, sir."

The technician took a tube of cold ooze and applied it to the electrodes at the end of long insulated wires. He placed one electrode on each of Pete's arms, one on each calf, and six on his midsection.

"This first one may startle you at first," the technician said, pushing a button labeled *FEAR*. "Relax. I just need to quickly calibrate our data to your emotions."

Pete felt a violent jolt of emotion burst from his heart and through his entire nervous system. An abstract sense of being trapped in the dark, like a caged animal, eaten alive. Fear. His whole body tied itself into a knot.

Like an electrical shock, the emotion of fear passed. The technician made a note of the graph paper's data as it spit out from the recorder.

"Shit!" Pete leaned forward, panting. "What the hell was that?"

"We just have a few more, sir. Please be patient. This next one will be infinitely more pleasant."

The technician pushed a button labeled *JOY*. Pete felt a tidal wave of emotion flow from his heart and into every corner of his body. An acute awareness of a brand new world without war, and a promising future for his unborn child. Joy. His whole body felt like warmed honey.

Like an electrical shock, the emotion of joy passed. The technician made a note of the graph paper's data.

"Wow," Pete said. "That was incredible. What is this machine?"

"Just a few more, sir."

The technician pushed a button labeled *SORROW*. Pete felt a ton of emotion hit his heart like a brick. A blunt sense of loss, sorrow, an abstract awareness of every friend he'd lost over the years. Complete and total sadness. His whole body ached.

Like an electrical shock, the emotion of sadness passed. The technician made a note of the graph paper's data.

"My God." Pete leaned forward and exhaled, wiping the tears from his eyes. "Please don't do that one again."

"Sit back, sir. You're going to love this one."

The technician pushed a button labeled *LOVE*. Pete felt an unstoppable hurricane of emotion explode from his heart, permeating every single cell of his body. It was the most beautiful feeling in the world, and he knew it well.

"Beatrice..."

Pete stood in a hall wearing only trousers and sweaty socks. A tray of his belongings waited for him atop another folding table.

"Did you bring me dinner?"

"What?" Pete said, disoriented.

A uniformed guard stood by the table and laughed, dropping a cigarette butt to the floor and snuffing it with his shoe. He exhaled two lungfuls of smoke and pointed to the foil-wrapped plate.

Pete stepped into his boots, slipped on his tank top and shirt, and dropped his keys and wallet into his pocket. "I've lost my appetite."

"Goop's cold, isn't it? Follow me."

Pete followed the guard down an arched passage of the underground complex toward the smell of gunpowder. Passing a perpendicular hall filled with cylindrical metal canisters, they zigzagged deeper into the facility before stopping at a door in the hall's concrete wall.

"I've been instructed to escort you out alone," the guard said, lighting another cigarette. "You can wash up and hit the head."

Dazed, Pete stood in a brightly lit latrine. Washbasins with shiny new hardware lined a mirrored wall.

What time is it?

A used straight razor sat unfolded at the edge of the first washbasin. Pete stared at it and pondered, his eyes empty, almost submissive. Picking it up by its cold wet blade, he pressed the sharp edge into his fingertip, slicing the flesh. The bead of blood became a warm trickle, running down his index finger and into the lines of his calloused palm.

Relax.

Pete dipped the corner of the razor's edge into the blood and smeared it across his wrist, creating a red pinstripe.

I just need to quickly calibrate our data to your emotions.

Snapping out of his trance, Pete dropped the razor and turned on the faucet, splashing water on his face, blowing his nose into his bloodied hands. Looking into the mirror, he thought he saw somebody behind him. He turned, but there was nobody there. He grabbed his chest.

CHAPTER FIFTEEN

PETE SLID DOWN THE HILLSIDE behind an abandoned guard shack at the bottom of an overgrown gully. A narrow chute -- a waterless well -- descended straight into the ground about thirty meters. Iron rungs bolted into the concrete wall served as a ladder down.

"This has to be it," Pete said. "Do me a favor and hold the light on me."

Mag clodhopped down the loose hill in his sandals, rucksack on his back.

"Hold on, brother..."

Pete dropped his rucksack to the ground and pulled out a crowbar, sharpened at one end, coated with decades of grime. Dropping it into the chute, he looked to the dark sky. He dropped his own flashlight into the large side pocket of his fatigues and stepped to the lip of the chute.

"Let's do this."

Pete jumped feet first into the mouth of the chute, freefalling into the deep darkness. Hitting the hard floor like a sack of potatoes, he got to his feet and shouted.

"LIGHT, PERRIER!!!"

Mag tossed his rucksack into the ivy and toed the rectangular chute's lip, shining the beam of his flashlight down into the earth. "You're thinking the book's down there?"

On the floor beneath Pete's boots was a thick steel manhole cover, partially covered with tumbleweeds and natural debris.

"It's connected to the battery," Pete called, his damp voice rising from the vertical chamber. "If I can get through here, we'll be on the other side of the two doors."

"I still gotta get Lucky Thirteen back by sunrise, brother. Quota, you know."

Pete picked up the crowbar from the chute's floor and cleared the manhole cover with his boots. Bracing his foot on the bottom rung, he wedged the crowbar into the sealed crevice of the manhole cover and pulled. Jammed.

Damn it.

Wedging the tip of the crowbar with his heel, Pete stepped up and forced his body weight downward to the chute's floor, trying to pry the manhole cover open. Teetering on the crowbar like a diver at the end of springboard, he placed his palms under a rung at eye level and pushed. Nothing.

Son of a...

Pete dug the flashlight out of his pocket and thumbed the switch, splashing the rusted manhole cover with light. Its round seal had been welded shut.

Read instructions.

Pete pulled Greamer's note out of his vest pocket and unfolded it, reviewing it under the light.

- - - - -

Read Instructions. Enigma.

Just

Know

Man

Never

Reverses

His

Choice.

133

Resolve,

His

Journey's

Key.

- - - - -

"What's going on down there, brother?"

Vexed, Pete grabbed the crowbar and slammed his anger against the manhole cover, the sound of metal on metal slicing up the chute and into the open night air.

"It's stuck," Pete hollered. "I can't open it." *Resolve, his journey's key --*

Mag held the light on the ladder.

The owl of gold. "Follow the dog..." The owl of gold.

Mag straddled the mouth of the chute, hunched over at the waist, fixing his beam upon Pete thirty meters below.

"Sun'll be coming up before you know it," Mag said. "I still gotta have Lucky Thirteen back to make my quota or Rip'll sling my ass."

Pete groaned at the bottom of the chute, scrunching the note in his fist, slamming his forehead against the wall.

Follow the dog.

"Where is he?" Pete shouted. "Where's Shadow?"

Mag didn't answer. The chute went black.

Pete shoved the balled note in his pocket. With the panic of a skin diver running out of air, he pocketed his flashlight and hurried back up the rungs of the dark chute toward open ground.

"Stay there, Perrier..."

Pete climbed like a rushed spider out of a drain, his shouts a cross between a drill sergeant and a used car salesman trying to close a deal.

"Shadow!" *This guy could take the dog right now and leave me down here.* "Little soldier..."

Mag pointed his flashlight at the ground. His adjusting eyes scaled the moonlit hillside of the brushy ravine, finding me a couple hundred meters away.

"Lucky Thirteen!" Mag shouted. "Whatcha got there, little brother?"

"Don't take him, Perrier..." Pete yelled from the chute, crawling up the rungs. "Don't take the dog. Just hold on..."

Distracted, Mag stepped from the chute and shined his light up the hill.

"PERRIER!!!"

"Get up here, brother. Looks like Lucky Thirteen's found something."

135

I dug as fast as I could into the wooded hillside, flinging mud and rocks through my hind legs into a scattered pile behind me. The delicious smell of dirt and pine needles became the smell of clay, followed by worms, slugs, roots, and paper. Layers beneath the faint smell of rotting lumber was a scent I did not know, driving me mad, getting stronger with every swipe of my paws.

CHAPTER SIXTEEN

WHILE OUR TROOPS SERVED in foreign lands during World War II, Pete served our country from Los Angeles, deep in the trenches of his mind. His war efforts at home were no less significant than those on the front lines. But as an underground codebreaker, he was sworn to secrecy, and unable to reveal the pivotal role he played in the Allied war effort. In the months that followed the war, like many men, Pete suffered bouts of depression, anxiety, paranoia, hallucinations, and other forms of post-war trauma.

The room was almost ready. The curtains matched the blankets to the carpet, the crib matched the rocker to the dresser. Stuffed toys sat in arranged rows waiting for the new arrival as the smells of glue and wood stain hung in the air.

"Is it getting better?"

Donna's gluey thumbs flattened out the final wet seam of bright blue-and-green wallpaper. A jungle pattern, with trees and monkeys and parrots and lions. She stood on a drop cloth and wore a loose smock with a gingham scarf around her head.

"Sometimes I feel like the war's not over," Beatrice said.

Beatrice finished placing folded miniature clothes into the dresser's organized drawers and sat down on the barely dry rocking chair. Her belly was the size of a basketball. Her pregnant ring finger wore the gold band, *DREAM TURNS*.

"That man *still* won't tell me everything. And he can't sleep."

It was the spring of 1946. I was just four years old in human years, and my soft puppy fuzz had given way to my coarse adult hair a couple years earlier. To occupy himself and leave the war behind, Pete had thrown himself into woodworking, spending all his energy preparing for the baby.

"Well, he's certainly found his calling," Donna said, admiring the crib's detailed rail. "Just gorgeous. Does he still work with dogs?"

"Not since the war," Beatrice said. "Spends all his time in the garage. Preparing for the baby. Filling orders..."

"Did you make an appointment?"

Beatrice rocked back and forth, hands on her belly, gazing out the window.

"He refuses to see a psychiatrist, Deedee. And it's getting worse. He throws screaming fits in the bathroom. And he keeps complaining of chest pains."

"HEY, BEA!!!"

Pete's shouts reverberated through our brand-new 1945 California bungalow with a slam of the back door.

"In here..."

Pete walked into the baby's room holding a stepladder in one hand and a contraption of wires in the other. Military fatigue pants and a ribbed tank top stuck to his skin with day-old sweat beneath an olive-drab assault vest loaded with pockets.

"All set," Pete said, positioning the ladder near the crib. "Ready for hanging. Hi Donna."

"Hi, honey," Donna said. "I love what you've done with the furniture. What's that?"

"A mobile." Pete stepped up to the ladder's third tread and reached for a single iron hook already screwed into the ceiling. "Made it from piano wires. Hobby store had all the thicknesses."

Pete lifted the half-assembled mobile above his head. Wires of various gauges and lengths dangled sloppily as he hung the main eighteen-inch section, positioning its center loop on the ceiling's hook.

"Cantilever effect." Stepping his boots up another tread, Pete braced himself with his dirty left palm flat against the ceiling and let the kinetic contraption hang balanced from his right thumb. "The trick is finding the center of gravity."

Pete placed the wiry parts in the empty crib and picked up the thickest eighteen-inch section. Bending it into a simple arc with his hands, he hung it back on the ceiling's hook by a center loop.

"A baby's vision is still developing in the crib," Pete said. "Simple shapes, high-contrast images, bold colors..."

Arced wire hanging in place, Pete reached into a vest pocket and pulled out two capital letters cut from colored card stock, each tied to a short length of string.

"She's getting a head start on colors and letters."

Pete hung a red letter *S* from the first looped end of the arced wire and an orange letter *H* from the other, allowing them to dangle freely by their strings.

"Going with the rainbow for her."

"Peter thinks it's a girl," Beatrice said.

"Never argue with a little girl's Papa," Donna said, leaving the baby's room and down the hall. "Let me fix you some lemonade, honeys."

Pete grabbed two more eighteen-inch lengths of wire from the crib and crisscrossed them with the first hung arced piece, forming a hub of six spokes. The apparatus hung from the ceiling like an umbrella frame.

"Two down." Pete blew at the red *S* and orange *H*, watching them flutter like wind chimes. "Four to go."

Four more bright letters followed: a yellow *A*, a green *D*, a blue *O*, and a purple *W*. Pete adjusted each of the strings and their positions so that they hung from the wire masterpiece in perfect balance.

S H A D O W

"Shadow the Strong," Beatrice said, reaching from her chair to pet me on the floor.

RIIINNNG. RIIINNNG --

The phone rang in the kitchen.

"Donna!" Pete called. "Can you get that?"

Pete pulled more thin wire through the ceiling's hook, lowering the mobile until the six letters hung just a few inches above the crib's decorative rail.

"It's beautiful," Beatrice said. "She's going to love it."

Donna walked back into the baby's room with two glasses of icy lemonade.

"Peter, it's a fellow named Charlie. He says it's urgent?"

"Chuck?" Pete stepped down to the wood floor with a heavy thump. "What's he want?"

Pete took a glass of lemonade from Donna and headed to the kitchen. Waiting for him to leave, Donna turned to Beatrice. Concerned.

"Just call and make the appointment," Donna said, handing her sister the glass. "I'll think up a way to get him down to the office."

Donna wiped her hands on a rag, admiring the creation suspended above the crib. She reached up and touched the dangling letters with her fingertips. "Oh, Shadow. How darling --"

"Bea..."

Pete walked back into the room.

"I have to go. That was somebody from intel."

"Intel?" Beatrice asked. "What for? You quit last year --"

Pete snapped.

"How many goddamn times do I have to tell you I can't talk about this stuff, Bea? How many times? How many years?"

Awkward silence. Donna wiped a spot on the floor.

"I'm taking Shadow with me," Pete said.

Beatrice stared at the floor. Pete apologized with a routine peck on the cheek.

"I'm sorry," Pete said. "I know, I know. You're right. I'm a son of a bitch."

"The mobile is just lovely," Donna said, rolling up a drop cloth.

"Thanks, Don. Do me a favor and look after your little sister while I'm gone. I'll call you two later."

CHAPTER SEVENTEEN

PETE'S EYES ADJUSTED to the darkness in a dive of all dives. A local watering hole, gushing with the stinky mélange of sweaty feet, body odor, stale beer, and cigarettes. With a plain sign outside simply reading *COCKTAILS*, it was the kind of place where nobody knew your name because it was better that way.

"Pete..."

Charlie sat at the end of the bar wearing a soiled coat and a fedora pulled down low. A notebook and Biro ballpoint pen sat on the bar in front of him next to a lowball glass of clear liquid.

"Sit down," Charlie said. "You alone?"

Ignoring the handful of other quiet faces drowning their pains, Pete waved the bartender off and gave Charlie a quick hug before pulling up a stool.

"My dog's outside. Been a long time, Chuck --"

"He never found you?"

It had been six months since Pete had seen Charlie face-to-face. The spectacled savant looked like he'd lost forty pounds and aged twenty years.

"Who?" Pete said. "You look like hell --"

Charlie opened the notebook in front of him. Smudgy sketches covered the pages: diagrams, numbers, dates, names, the kind of demented doodles you'd expect to see in the journal of a madman.

"What's this about?" Pete asked, looking at the notebook.

"Quiet," Charlie whispered, grabbing Pete's wrist. "He's telling me to do it."

"Do what? Who? You're shaking, man --"

"He's made the others do it too."

"What?" Pete repeated. "Who did?"

"Now I need to do it," Charlie mumbled, raising his glass to his flaked lips. Charlie began raising his voice, digging his fingernails into Pete's forearm. Heads turned. "He says so."

"What the fuck are you talking about?" Pete pulled his arm away and stood from his stool.

Charlie looked around the room through his thick spectacles and shivered.

"Sit down," Charlie said. "He gave me some keys. Look."

"Who did?"

"Greamer."

"Greamer? The agent from the debriefing?"

"Yeah."

Charlie pointed to the top corner of an ink-covered page in the notebook. Etched into the paper in dark ink was a series of anagrammatic phrases.

THY BAD SEEDING

HAND BEGS DEITY

BENIGHTED DAYS

DENY THIS BADGE

ANY DEBT HE DIGS

BAD EYED THINGS

BY HIDDEN GATES

Pete read the phrases in silence.

"Switch the letters around," Charlie said.

"*Death by design*?" Pete blurted.

"You got it. *Death by design*. Greamer has it out for us. A grudge. He says we interfered with his design."

"Design? What kind of design?"

"He told me the death toll from the war was his idea." Charlie pushed his thick glasses up the bridge of his nose. "He said we got in the way."

"Do you realize how insane you sound right now?"

Charlie flipped to another page full of jotted names, most of them crossed out with dates beside them.

"These are the codebreakers that were at the meeting," Charlie said. "I lifted the list from an officer later that night."

Several dozen crossed-out names were scribbled down the page in two columns. *Francesca Allen, William Bryan, Stanley Davis...*

Pete's eyes skimmed the list of crossed-out names.

"You're just tired, Chuck. Why don't you come on over to the house. Bea's sister is there. We'll have some dinner --"

"They're dead," Charlie said. "They all did it. Greamer told them to..."

Charlie flipped the dog-eared page, revealing more crossed-out names. He looked around the room from under his fedora.

"I've been keeping tabs on everybody since then," Charlie said. "Had to crack into some public records to pull the addresses. Andreas hanged himself. One woman gassed herself in the oven. Just last week, that fisherman? He locked himself in the garage and started his car..."

"I think you need some rest, Chuck --"

"He hasn't found you yet?"

Charlie turned to a page of handwritten graphs, lists, diagrams, and numbers. Pete looked closer.

"You say Greamer is behind all this. Why?"

"Because he's mad, that's why."

Charlie began writing out a line of numbers in a sequence at the bottom of the page.

"Greamer has a death wish on any codebreaker," Charlie said. "His hit list. But he's making us do it ourselves..."

Pete rested his hand on Charlie's back.

"What about the police?"

"We can't go to them," Charlie said, his face turning to stone. "We have to do it ourselves. I have to do it --"

Do what? "Take a deep breath," Pete said. "Relax, I'm gonna get us a round --"

"NO!!!" Charlie stood from his stool, a pistol tucked in his belt.

Pete tried to remain calm.

"Settle down," Pete said. "Before somebody calls the police. And hide that piece."

"It's over," Charlie whispered. "He got us..."

"Take it easy."

Pete flagged the bartender. It took a moment to get his attention.

"What can I do you for?" the bartender said.

"Two beers."

Pete turned to face Charlie and saw only the notebook and Biro pen sitting in front of an empty barstool. He grabbed the pen and began scribbling spirals on a napkin until he struck ink.

Death by design?

Pete wrote three words on the napkin.

DEATH BY DESIGN

Pete stared at the napkin, his imagination turning the inked letters upside-down and sideways, flipping them, stacking them, rolling them, back and forth, shuffling them, tossing them in the air to let them fall where they may in the abyss of his consciousness.

He stopped and looked up at the bartender.

"Hey, pal, what time did my buddy come in here? The kid with the hat and glasses --"

POP!!!

A gunshot rang out from the back of the barroom.

Pete barged into the small windowless lavatory at the back of the barroom. Blood splattered the mirror. Charlie lay on the floor, gun in hand, a bullet in his head.

"Chuck!"

Pete dropped to his knees and rolled Charlie onto his back. Blood gushed from his temple. Pete checked for a pulse.

"One to go," a raspy voice said. Pete's leg hair stood up. He sprang to his feet and looked around the empty lavatory.

"Who's there?"

There was nobody there. Pete dropped to his knee and put his ear to Charlie's chest. Nothing. Charlie was gone.

"He did well," the raspy voice said. "As ordered. You're next, Sergeant."

Spooked out of his skin, Pete jumped up and looked around the small lavatory. There was nobody there.

He turned to the sink and looked in the mirror. Rip Greamer was standing behind him.

"Jesus Christ!"

Pete spun around. There was nobody there. He spun back to face the mirror. Greamer stood behind him, stirring black coffee with a knife. They locked eyes in the mirror.

"It's time we talk about my quota, Sergeant. The quota you disrupted."

Pete turned once more. Nobody there. He turned to face the mirror, adrenaline pumping through his soul. Greamer glared at him over his shoulder through the mirror.

"I thought I was just going insane," Pete said.

"Oh, but you are, Sergeant."

Greamer pressed the knife's edge into his pasty tongue.

"You're the agent at H.Q. --"

"Your colleagues have all done what I've asked of them. You're the last one. What has taken you so long, Sergeant?"

Pete looked down at his fallen friend, blood running from his head. "What have you done to him?"

"I drove him to do it himself, of course. A more creatively fulfilling way to balance my quota. The quota you ruined, Sergeant."

Pete looked back in the mirror, his eyes watering.

"Quota?"

"The numbers, Sergeant. The books. The souls you robbed from me. You ended the war. My design."

"But..."

"Call it a grudge, Sergeant."

Pete leaned into the mirror and shouted.

"A grudge for what? For what we did? For cracking codes? For ending the war? For saving the world?"

Greamer ran the tip of his knife along the edge of Pete's right ear.

"I hold no grudge against the minds that *could*, Sergeant. I hold a grudge against the hearts that *would*."

Pete grabbed his chest, scrunching his vest in his grip.

"Yes, Sergeant. Your heart. It's that thing beating in your chest. That piece of meat that controls your emotions. I know everything about it."

Greamer breathed down Pete's neck.

Authenticating my vitals...

153

"I know what makes you tick," Greamer continued. "I'll make you do it."

Pete shook his head.

"Never!"

"My quota has one more slot to be filled, Sergeant. A slot reserved for you."

Pete shook his head like a man trying to wake up.

"Why haven't you just had me killed?"

"You mean murder? I'm an artist, Sergeant. Murder is effective, but too easy. It lacks poetry. Boring. Driving you to suicide, however, is a challenge. And I enjoy a challenge."

Pete's face was defiant.

"No way. I'll never do it. I'll never leave her."

Greamer breathed down Pete's neck and smiled.

"Beatrice, is it? And her unborn?"

"No..." Pete whispered, staring at the beast behind him in the mirror.

Greamer planted his knife in his coffee and pulled out a handheld device. He read the display and nodded.

"You know, technically I can fill your slot with any soul of my choosing. I see Beatrice Durante gives me two for the price of one. That's even better."

Greamer snickered. Something had dawned on him.

"Of course," Greamer continued. "Forget about our meeting today. I'll just take Beatrice. One more soul is all I need for this round."

"No! Leave her alone!"

"You've saved yourself, Sergeant. Congratulations."

Pete punched the mirror, its shards falling into the sink.

"WHAT WAS THAT?!?" The bartender plowed into the lavatory, tripping over Charlie's body. He gasped at the sight of blood on Pete's hands. "WHAT IN GOD'S NAME?!?"

Pete turned for the door and fled the lavatory.

CHAPTER EIGHTEEN

DONNA PUT THE SKILLET on the oven's center rack. A browned roast, seasoned with salt and pepper, laced with a clove of garlic and chunks of carrots, potatoes, and onions. Adding a cup of broth and covering the dish, she closed the oven and set it on a low heat.

"The war did that to a lot of men," Donna said. "It's best not to take it personally."

Beatrice sat in the dining chair facing the window, watching the grey marine layer roll in from the coastal bluffs beyond the backyard lawn.

"It's starting to rain."

RIIINNNG. RIIINNNG --

Donna picked up the phone...

"Donna, it's Pete."

I waited outside the isolated phone booth, located in a desolate city park just a block away from the point.

"No!" Pete screamed into the phone, dehydrated. "I need to talk to you. Has anybody come by the house?"

Pete's voice squeaked out between stuttering breaths. I could feel his heart beating faster than a hummingbird's.

"Has anybody called?"

The phone booth's glass windows began to fog.

"There's somebody looking for me..."

Pete wiped the phone booth's foggy windows with his bloody knuckles, peering outside in all four directions.

"No, not a shrink. I think he's using some kind of psycho-triangulation. He's finding all of us. He's dangerous..."

A curious crow looked down upon us, perched on a wire.

"For what we did during the war. I need you to take your sister to your place. Right now, Donna. Get her out of the house. But don't tell her why."

Pete paused, listening.

"The less she knows, the better. Try and keep her calm."

Pete nodded, looking through the glass.

"A dangerous man. Name's Greamer. Definitely not one of us. He's looking for me, and now I think he wants her too..."

Pete took a deep breath.

"No!" Pete explained. "No police! Even the Black Chamber is in cahoots with this guy."

Pete spoke softer.

"I can't come home. He'll follow me."

Pete began to shout, dancing in the tight phone booth with an anxious stupor.

"Listen, Don..."

Pete calmed down.

"You girls get over to your place. Make sure you're not followed. When you get there, call Naylor. Bea knows the number."

Pete wiped the fogged glass with his fist and spoke as clearly as possible.

"Tell Naylor I found something with Shadow at the point. Tell him it's something he needs to see. The point. He needs to come right away. Call Naylor."

Pete nodded.

"But get your sister to your place before you do anything. Lock the doors, and don't answer the phone. Not until you talk to Naylor."

Pete flattened his hand against the glass and listened. He paused.

"Just tell her not to forget what I always told her. And Donna…"

Pete froze in the phone booth.

"Please hurry."

Pete slammed the phone on its hook and stepped out of the booth into the drizzle.

"Let's go, little soldier."

We left the phone booth on foot, making the short trek to the coastline's ridge. The rain began to fall hard. Pete contemplated out loud.

"If I don't do this, he'll take both of them. I live, they die. Where would that leave us, little soldier? I have no choice. He'll take them if I don't…"

Coves and bluffs ran along the San Pedro shoreline, its vertical cliffs falling straight down 120 feet to the ruthless surf below. The ridge led to the lighthouse's rocky point, jutting out into the cold Pacific.

"It'll look like an accident," Pete said as we trudged through the young mud. "They'll be taken care of for the rest of their lives if it's an accident. And she'll have Donna. She'll move on. She'll be fine."

Pete looked out to sea as we reached the lighthouse.

"But I need you to take care of them too."

The most important job of my life was about to begin.

"It's what I have to do, little soldier. Tell her everything. She'll understand some day."

Pete led me to the other side of the lighthouse, a few feet from the cliff's edge. He took a knee in the mud and checked my tags through pellets of rain.

"Naylor will be here soon. Stay, and wait for Naylor."

Pete stood, grabbing my muzzle, looking me in the eyes. Rain ran down his bare arms.

"You got that, little soldier?"

Consider it done.

"Sit."

Pete walked to the edge and faced the sea. Rain and Pacific surf pounded the jagged rocks below. His voice lowered.

"Stay."

And so I sat there, alone, like a statue in the rain. Staying.

CHAPTER NINETEEN

ROTTING LEAVES, snail shells, potato bugs, and slumbering beetles flew through my hind legs as I dug like a Chinese mole in a hurry to get home. Stopping only for a moment to sneeze away the mud that clogged my nostrils, I went back to work, vertical, my head burrowing its way into the hollowness that waited for us beneath the hillside.

"Lucky Thirteen's found something, brother."

Mag dropped his rucksack to the ground and circled around the sinkhole, shining his light on my work.

"Looks like some sort of caved-in bunker."

Pete sprinted up the hill from the chute. Tossing his rucksack aside, he stood at the edge of the neck-deep sinkhole and looked down at my discovery.

"Sinkhole," Pete said, looking at his watch. "Off, little soldier."

I stopped digging and backed away from my masterpiece, rabid with curiosity, resisting the magnetic scent that oozed from the fissure in the hillside. The moist ground had already caved in several feet from the ground's surface after more than a half-century of heavy rains.

"Hold the light on it, Perrier."

Pete sat at the edge of the sinkhole, his legs dangling down mud walls lined with twisted roots and eras of erosion.

"Outta here for a second, little soldier. Out!"

I jumped out of the sinkhole and sat next to Mag at the edge.

"Lucky Thirteen," Mag whispered. "Nicely done, Lucky Thirteen. Couldn't find it without you."

Pete stepped down into the sinkhole, bracing himself on the edge with his hands, carefully committing his body's weight to the crumbling floor. He crouched with his flashlight, squinting into the caved-in opening in the hillside. Splintered lumber.

"Redwood shoring. Give me a shovel."

Pete stood eye-level with us and stomped his boot, the collapsing earth giving way. Mag rummaged through his rucksack and unfolded a shovel, handing it down. Pete jabbed the shovel like a spade into the hole's floor, chipping away at its edges. Dirt fell through the crack, like sand through an hourglass.

"It's the shaft," Pete said. "The tunnel shaft."

Pete pounded his heels downward, sweeping dirt away with his boots, exposing heavy wood beams beneath the floor of the sinkhole.

"These them, brother? Rip's tunnels?"

"Yep. We're going in through the ceiling."

Mag patted the top of my head, shining his flashlight upon my master. "You are one lucky dog. Ready to take us to the book?"

Pete kicked at the rift in the sinkhole's floor, creating an opening just large enough for a grown man to wriggle through.

"Give me a headlamp, Perrier. In my bag."

Pete hunched over the open hole, grasping a loose root in the sinkhole's dirt wall, shining his hand-held flashlight into the open void at his feet. Mag pulled a headlamp from the bag and handed it down.

"And the rope..."

Pete stood like a pair of open scissors in the sinkhole and loaded the headlamp with batteries, fixing it around his head like a miner. The distant sound of falling dirt and rocks pattered below him.

"In my bag. Tie it to that tree."

Mag got to his feet and pulled a coil of rope from one of the rucksacks, tying it awkwardly around a tree behind him. He turned and tossed the coil down to Pete.

"Pull on it," Pete said. "Tight?"

Mag pulled the rope taut with his thick leathery hands, its tangled knot gripping the trunk of the tree.

"As a frog's ass, brother."

Pete dropped the end of the rope into the dark gap in the hillside, feeding coils of slack into the unseen chasm below. He held the rope in his palms and got on his backside, sliding feet-first into the airy darkness. I tried to follow.

"Stay, little soldier."

Pete disappeared into the ground.

"What do you see down there, brother?"

Mag crouched at the edge of the hole with my head in his huge hand.

"How deep is it?"

The rope went limp, its slack drooping to the ground from the tree.

166

"Pete?"

The rope tightened again, going up like a diagonal clothesline. Pete stuck his dusty head out of the floor of the sinkhole, his headlamp shining in our eyes.

"Give me the bags."

Mag picked up a rucksack in each hand and handed them down.

"You're next, little soldier."

Pete slid the bags through the sinkhole and into the darkness below.

"Give me a hand with the dog, man. And keep that rope tied. It's deeper than I thought."

Mag knelt at the edge of the sinkhole and cradled me in his thick arms.

"Let's go, Lucky Thirteen. Attaboy. Go help Daddy find that *Triad of Hell.*"

Pete held the rope with his left hand and took me against his ribs. I did my best to relax.

"You ready to get your nose into some weird shit?"

Pete yanked once more on the taut rope. I held my breath...

Pete's boots broke our fall. We stumbled atop the bags on the floor of a narrow tunnel, sandwiched by complete darkness in both directions. Wood pillars supported the top of the corridor along open dirt walls, with vertical beams buckling beneath the weight of the dirt ceiling. Electrical wiring that had long since stopped functioning dangled from above. The scent, almost metallic, was getting stronger.

Releasing me, Pete shined his light at the hole in the dirt ceiling and pulled on the rope.

"Let's go, Perrier --"

Sliding through the hole of the collapsing ceiling, Mag thumped to the tunnel floor in a deluge of dirt and rubble. Getting to his feet, face covered in dust, he picked up a rucksack and shined his light down the creaky wood-beamed passage and into the black.

Pete laughed. "You look like a ghost."

Mag brushed his face with his rough palms, shaking out his poncho, his flashlight's beam cutting through the soup of dust that hung in the air of the tunnel. He looked up and blinked, like a man with loose contact lenses.

"A place only a dog could find. How deep are we, brother?"

"About fifteen feet."

Mag slung his rucksack over his broad shoulder.

"The perfect depth for two and a half dead men. Just you and us, Lucky Thirteen!"

Pete hunched over his rucksack and pulled out a second headlamp, loading it with batteries. He turned it on.

"Put this on," Pete said. "You're going to need your hands."

Mag fitted the lamp on his head and turned back to the sinkhole.

"We need the rope, brother?"

"We have more."

Pete regrouped, folding the shovel and shoving it into his rucksack. Standing up, he slapped the rest of the batteries in his vest pockets and pulled out his compass.

"This way..."

I took point and followed the scent, leading us single-file down the narrow shaft, the guys lighting the way behind me with their headlamps. Decayed joists, electrical wiring, and tangled roots hung from the dirt ceiling above their heads, reinforced by chewed wood beams. We walked down the tunnel as if it were a minefield, its floor riddled with fallen debris. Pete followed tightly on my tail. Mag brought up the rear.

"Let's find that *Triad of Hell*, Lucky Thirteen."

Hanging a sharp right through a collapsing doorway, I took us into a small room off the main shaft, set up like an office. Pete shouted and ran past me toward a dinged metal supply cabinet in the corner, coated with decades of dust, its door ajar.

"In here."

Pete swung open the thin metal door, his headlamp shining into the cabinet. Two black eyes stared back at him, their icy glare spewing a furious gust of wind across the room.

"Shit --"

I barked, lunging at the monster as it squawked in a fluster. Pete jerked, falling back toward the doorway, the creature bouncing off the office walls. Flying past Pete's head and scraping his cheek, it flew out the office door and disappeared down the shaft and into the blackness.

"Christ."

Pete sat panting on the floor of the office, his back against the wall. Mag walked into the office from the main shaft.

"What was that thing, brother? I felt it go right by me --"

"Fucking owl. And not *the owl of gold*."

"Who?" Mag laughed at his own cheap joke and looked around, his headlamp illuminating the corners of the room. "This an office?"

Pete got to his feet and walked to a medium-sized metal footlocker sitting on the corner desk. Swiping debris off its surface with his bare forearm, he opened the case's unlocked latch and lifted the lid.

"Here we go..."

Pete reached into the footlocker and pulled out a long scroll of paper, clean, the size of a large rolled up poster.

"Now we're talking."

Pete unrolled a large architectural map, flattening it with his arms on the desk. Mag whispered in awe, staring at the flattened map of corridors, passages, rooms, and halls.

"Blueprints, brother? Maps?"

"Tunnel plans," Pete said, wiping his nose with his knuckles.

Mag hunched over Pete's shoulder as they both examined the large schematics under their headlamps. Channels and exits, openings and pathways, all charted out on paper, labeled by hand. Red pencil markings with dates had been written on the plans.

"*Harbor Defenses of Los Angeles*," Mag said, reading the labels aloud from the map. "*Kitchen. Communications Hall. Office of the Post Engineer.* How old is this place, brother?"

Mag set his rucksack on the desk.

"Nineteen forty-four."

Pete flattened out the corner of the map, running his fingertips along the drafting lines. His finger stopped, pointing to a location on the map.

"That's where we need to be."

Pete rolled up the map, folded it, and jammed it into a vest pocket. He looked at his watch.

"*Follow the dog.*"

I led us out of the office and down the dark corridor, the dank scent growing stronger than ever.

CHAPTER TWENTY

GREAMER STOOD at the lip of the Pacific, its salty tongue lapping at his feet. Rain pelted the draping black hooded parka that shrouded his vileness, the fingers of his right hand pushing the buttons of a handheld device in a smooth fury.

"How dare you, Sergeant? How dare you cut in line? It only makes my job more difficult."

Clutching his bottomless thermos of black coffee in his left hand, Greamer stood over Pete, spewing hellish vapors of chagrin. His dark eyes smoldered through the tint of his glasses.

"When you make my design your own, you disrespect me as an artist, Sergeant."

Chest down, face up, body shattered. Pete looked into the falling rain and said nothing, his shell splayed on the mollusk-encrusted rocks that kissed the bluff. Conscious, yet no longer able to smell the stench of life in the tide.

Am I dead? Pete opened his mouth, vomiting silence.

The gangling beast sipped his coffee, spindling at the buttons of his device with demon-like proficiency.

"I hate cheaters, Sergeant."

Pete's gasp finally found the rain. "Beatrice --"

"Choosing to jump in order to protect your wife and child is a noble idea, Sergeant. Clever. But you can't fool me."

"Beatrice --"

"Did you really think you could outsmart *me*?"

"Where is she?" Pete said, body broken.

Greamer circled Pete's mangled shell, reading his device.

"Did you really think you could save them by choosing suicide, Sergeant? What kind of artist do you think I am? Your suicide was to be *my* choice. Not yours. You've gone and filled *my* quota on *your* terms."

Greamer scowled in the rain.

"You haven't fooled anybody, Sergeant Durante."

Pete felt nothing below his eyes.

"This is *my* design," Greamer said, bony arm pointing along the grey horizon. "*Not yours.*"

Greamer rubbed his jaw, rain dripping from the edge of his black hood.

"But I must admit you've got quite a right hook. If I do say so myself."

Greamer circled Pete like a bored wolf finding a carcass.

"You were quite the puzzle solver, Sergeant. A true master of the codebreaking craft. But your art ultimately interfered with mine."

Greamer held his knife like a pen in his fingers.

"Where is she?" Pete asked.

Greamer held his smarmy grin to the sky, rain bouncing off his glasses and down his jaundiced face.

"You know, Sergeant, I've always loved playing games in the rain."

Greamer paused and looked at his device.

"I have an idea," Greamer said. "Stand up."

Pete's body twitched, sharp passing pains of reality searing into his brain. Joints found sockets while fractures mended themselves beneath his flesh. His neck twisted 180 degrees as he stood, his limbs intact, his body in perfect shape. His eyes blinked as they met Greamer's behind the tinted thick-rimmed spectacles.

Pete took inventory of his body, confused. He moved his fingers, he shook his arms. Greamer looked him up and down with a malicious grin and pulled out a sealed white envelope from his parka. He handed it to Pete.

"Your suicide has been denied."

Pete felt neither alive nor dead. He wiggled his fingers, clenching and unclenching his fists, feeling his wrist for a pulse. He stared at the envelope in his hand.

"Where is she --"

"A good artist never shares his secrets, Sergeant."

Greamer took a swig of coffee and vanished.

CHAPTER TWENTY-ONE

SECRET WRITING, or cryptography, is the practice and study of disguising a message in order to make it unreadable by potential interceptors or eavesdroppers. Through a process called encryption, an ordinary message is first converted into gibberish using a cipher, or a key. For a human to understand the message, he must decipher the information, converting the gibberish back into a readable message.

Many encryption devices have been designed throughout Man's history in order to facilitate secret communication, from the ancient Greek scytale to the digital signatures used on the Internet today. One of the most famous encryption machines is the Enigma machine, invented by a German engineer and used by Nazi Germany to encrypt military communication before and during World War II. The Germans placed lots of confidence in the security of the Enigma, and considered its encrypted messages too sophisticated to be decrypted by their enemies.

They were wrong. Led by a British genius named Alan Turing, an elite group of minds worked together behind closed doors to successfully reverse-engineer the Enigma system, figuring out how the machine worked. Critical Nazi messages were intercepted by the Allies and deciphered by these brilliant minds, ultimately leading to the fall of the Nazi regime and the Axis powers.

Mag followed me into a communications room behind an open steel door down the main underground corridor, a few hundred meters north of the sinkhole. Redwood beams struggled responsibly to keep the ceiling from caving in, buckling like elbows beneath the weight of the earth above.

"What have we here, Lucky Thirteen?"

I took a quick inventory of room, sniffing out the corners where the dirt walls met the floor. A smell of live electronics stood poised with rows of corroding consoles and chairs facing a large projector screen against the far wall. Pete entered from the main shaft.

"Son of a bitch. Enigma --"

Pete walked over to join Mag at a machine sitting atop a long desk at the back of the room. It looked a lot like a typewriter.

"Ain't that like the one in your garage, brother?"

"Yeah, but this one only has three rotors."

Pete dropped his rucksack and sat down on the chair in front of the Enigma machine. It had several components, including a plug board, a light board, a keyboard, and a set of three rotors.

"I never worked with this model before..."

Pete looked over the machine like a nostalgic old man finding a forgotten toy train set in the attic, running the tip of his calloused thumb across the three rotors already set to *A-A-A*.

"Rotor settings are the first part of encrypting with the Enigma. This one only has three."

Pete spun the rightmost rotor, rotating it like the wheel of an odometer, one click at a time. *A-A-B... A-A-C...*

"Each rotor is mapped to the twenty-six letters of the alphabet."

Pete moved the rightmost rotor one more click. *A-A-D...*

"Just like the odometer in your van, but the wheels go from *A* through *Z* instead of *zero* through *nine*.

The odometer's on a base-ten system. Think of these Enigma rotors as a base-twenty-six system. But with only three wheels."

Mag leaned over the machine, reading the rotors with his headlamp.

"So how were the bad guys sending their secret messages?"

"To decrypt a message, they'd enter a string of letters using the keyboard here."

Pete grazed his fingertips over the keyboard.

"When they typed a letter in, the Enigma gave them a new encoded letter with these lights. One letter at a time."

Pete adjusted his headlamp.

"When you press a key on the keyboard, an electrical current flows through the machine and lights up one of these letters. There's a bulb under each one."

Pete ran his fingernails across the letters on the light board.

"The lit letter is the secret letter."

Pete checked the back of the machine.

"Holy shit, Perrier. He left it on for us."

"Who? Rip?"

"Somebody worse."

Pete sat back down and typed out a string of letters, illuminating letters on the light board.

"Yes..."

Pete used his thumbs to set the three rotors, cycling them one click at a time. *D-O-G.* He reset them back to *A-A-A.*

"These three wheels rotate one click every time you hit a key on the keyboard."

Pete cracked his knuckles, launching a crash course in Enigma cryptanalysis into Mag's face.

"Whatever the sender sets the rotors to will determine the algorithm for the message. That's the key. The recipient of the code just needs to set up his machine exactly the same way. With the same key."

Pete hit a key on the keyboard. The rightmost rotor rotated a single click. *A-A-B.*

"Just like your odometer, the right wheel will cycle all the way through, twenty-six times. After a full rotation, the middle wheel will start moving. One click at a time."

"Like the tenths of a mile."

"Exactly. But base-twenty-six."

Pete leaned forward with his mouth on his fist, chewing his knuckles, staring at the machine.

181

"I need the rotor settings."

Sitting up in his chair, Pete spun the three rotors with both thumbs, setting different combinations. *A-B-C. X-Y-Z. U-S-A.* He reset them back to *A-A-A.*

"This the way to the *Triad of Hell*, brother?"

Pete visited his thoughts alone, messing with the machine, spinning the rotors, hitting keys. With each press of a key on the keyboard, a corresponding letter would illuminate on the light board.

"I just need the key," Pete mumbled. "I can't do anything without the key."

"How about the maps, brother? Maybe they're a clue?"

Pete hung his head in silence, his headlamp shining into his lap.

Resolve, his journey's key.

Pete gasped. Digging into his pocket, he pulled out the note from Greamer and flattened it out on the table beside the Enigma machine.

- - - - -

Read Instructions. Enigma.

Just

Know

Man

Never

Reverses

His

Choice.

Resolve,

His

Journey's

Key.

- - - - -

Pete slapped the note.

"The key. Of course. This is the key --"

"*Read Instructions*," Mag said, reading from the note. "*Enigma*. Type it in, brother!"

Pete smiled, counting the words on the note. He nodded, pointing to the three rotors on the machine.

A-A-A

"I need to set the rotors first. Watch this..."

Pete ticked the leftmost rotor and glanced down at the note. *Read Instructions. Enigma.*

"*Read --*"

Pete stopped the first rotor on the letter *R.*

R-A-A

Pete ticked the middle rotor and stopped it on *I*. *Instructions.*

"*Instructions --*"

R-I-A

"*Air?*" Mag offered, enthralled. "*Air* backwards?"

"*R-I-A* is an anagram for *air*. But, no --"

Pete ticked the rightmost rotor with his thumb. *Enigma. E.*

"*E,*" Pete said. "*E* for *Enigma.*"

R-I-E

"*Read Instructions,*" Pete said. "*Enigma. R-I-E.* That's our key."

"That rhymes, brother."

Pete reached into a vest pocket and took out a Biro ballpoint pen and the cardboard backing of an empty battery package, slapping them on the table in front of Mag. He sat at the machine with both hands, like a jittery kid ready to beat his own high score on an arcade game.

"Here, write these down. I'm going to read them one at a time."

Mag put on his game face and took the pen, scribbling spirals on the back of the empty battery package until he struck ink.

"Go ahead, brother."

"One letter at a time," Pete repeated. "I'll read you a letter, you write it down. Don't look at what I'm doing or you'll get confused."

"Got it, brother. Go ahead."

Pete stretched his left fingers along the edge of Greamer's note, reading to himself by his headlamp.

Just Know Man Never Reverses His Choice. Resolve, His Journey's Key. J-K-M-N-R-H-C-R-H-J-K.

"Okay, man. Here we go..."

Just. J. Pete positioned his right hand over the machine's keyboard and pressed the letter *J* with his index finger. Two things happened. First, the rightmost rotor rotated one click, to *F. R-I-F.* Second, the letter *A* lit up on the machine's light board.

"*A*," Pete said aloud, reading the illuminated letter on the machine's light board.

"*A*," Mag repeated, writing the letter down.

Know. K. Pete positioned his right hand over the machine's keyboard and pressed the letter *K* with his index finger. Two things happened. First, the rightmost rotor rotated one click, to *G. R-I-G.* Second, the letter *N* lit up on the machine's light board.

"*N*," Pete said aloud, reading the illuminated letter on the machine's light board.

"*N*," Mag repeated, writing the letter down.

Pete continued studying Greamer's note in silence, entering the first capital letter from each word on the note using the machine's keyboard. With each entry, the rightmost rotor clicked to its next letter, and a corresponding letter illuminated on the light board.

Man. M. Pete hit the letter *M* on the keyboard, lighting up the letter *G* on the light board.

"*G*," Pete said, reading the illuminated letter.

"*G*," Mag repeated, writing the letter down.

Never. N. Pete hit the letter *N* on the keyboard, lighting up the letter *L* on the light board.

"*L*," Pete said aloud, reading the illuminated letter.

"*L*," Mag repeated, writing the letter down.

Reverses. R. Pete hit the letter *R* on the keyboard, lighting up the letter *E* on the light board.

"*E*," Pete said aloud, reading the illuminated letter.

"*E*," Mag repeated, writing the letter down.

J-K-M-N-R-H-C-R-H-J-K. Pete continued pressing each letter on the keyboard one at a time, voicing its corresponding letter as it lit up on the light board. Mag wrote them down.

"...S," Pete said aloud, reading the illuminated letter.

"S," Mag repeated, writing the letter down.

Eleven letters total. Done.

"That's it," Pete said.

"*Angled runes?*" Mag stood back, reading his writing under his headlamp. "*Angled runes.*"

Pete stood from the machine and turned his attention to what Mag had written down.

A-N-G-L-E-D-R-U-N-E-S

"*Angled runes,*" Pete repeated aloud. *Runes?* Pete stared at Mag's chicken-scratch handwriting on the back of the battery package and paced the room.

"What are *runes*, brother?"

"Letters in an ancient alphabet. A runic alphabet." It was something Pete knew.

"*Angled runes,*" Mag mumbled, pondering. Lost.

That's odd. Pete looked up to the dirt ceiling and walked back to the machine. "The runic alphabets used angular shapes for their letters."

"What language?"

"I don't think it's talking about the letters themselves," Pete continued. "Hmmm..."

"What then?"

"Runes are not only letters of an alphabet, but types of codes."

Pete talked his way through a revelation.

"*Runes. Angled.* But not geometric angles. *Angled runes* isn't talking about the shape of the letters. It's talking about encrypted lines. Or secret perspectives. *Angled.* Like, *slanted. Angled runes.* Like, *slanted messages.* Formed codes. Twisted words. *Angled runes.*"

Mag rubbed his eyes.

"That's pretty deep, brother."

"Wordplay. It's a natural form of encryption."

"You sure you did it right?"

"Greamer told me I'd understand when I see him again."

Pete stood over the Enigma machine and stared at it under his headlamp, listening to Greamer's abrasive voice in his head.

You'll understand when you see me again, Sergeant. I assure you. Turn repeated.

Pete pointed to the three rotors on the machine.

"Look."

Mag circled around the table and examined the rotor settings.

R-I-P

CHAPTER TWENTY-TWO

QUIETLY I SAT THERE, alone at the top of the cliff, wolfing down the stench of the withdrawing tide. The rain had stopped. I was on full alert, waiting for Pete as he scaled the cliff like a crab, his fingertips filling crevices in the bluff's craggy wall.

Beatrice --

The loose wall beneath Pete's left boot gave way, sending his body spiraling down to the jagged beach below. His shell bounced like a mannequin across the crusty rocks, rolling into the slippery pools that remained from the visiting tide. Unharmed, he stood to his feet in the wet field of shellfish and seaweed and looked up to the clearing sky.

"LITTLE SOLDIER!!!"

Pete felt his wrist for a pulse. Nothing. He held his fingertips to his neck. Nothing. He held his palm to his chest. No heartbeat at all. No pain, no blood, no injury. Yet very much alive.

"LITTLE SOLDIER!!!" Pete shouted from the beach. *Stay there, boy...*

Pete climbed back up the 120-foot cliff in a new kind of panic.

Beatrice --

A helicopter circled the point like a steel vulture, the sound of its propeller reflecting off the surf and up from the rocks below. Its giant illuminated eye scanned the beach in the darkening sky as Pete pulled his muddy body up from the ledge and rolled to his side in front of me. Exhaling, he got to his feet in a hurry.

"Little soldier --"

Pete looked off the edge of the cliff at the helicopter descending to the beach, feeling his wrist once more for a pulse. Nothing. Taking a knee in front of me, he held my head in his hands, looking me in the eyes. He smelled different.

"Change of plans, Shadow. We've got to get home to our girls."

Pete led me on our hike from the point back to the house, leaving the sound of the chopper and sirens behind. We walked faster than usual, the dusk's horizon turning from blue to orange.

"She's at Donna's," Pete said, looking straight ahead, holding his palm to his chest. "She has to be at Donna's." *Please, God. Let her be safe.*

Pete took Greamer's envelope from a vest pocket and unfolded it in his hands. Branded into the envelope, inkless:

PETER DURANTE

Pete broke the seal, pulling out a crisp white note. On it were three words. Inkless, yet readable:

— — — — —

MORE MERCY GONE

— — — — —

"*Mercy*," Pete mumbled, shoving the note back into his vest pocket. *Beatrice --*

We turned left up our quiet street, walked past the houses of our neighbors, and reached our driveway. Pete sprinted to the front porch.

"Bea!"

Unlocked.

Pete swung the front door open and ran into the living room.

"Bea! Babe!"

Silence.

"Donna? I'm back..."

Silence.

"Hello?"

Pete ran into the bedroom. Just the bed, unmade. *Bea?* He ran into the baby's room. The hanging mobile waited alone. He turned and ran into the bathroom, throwing the shower curtain aside with a swipe of his arm. Nothing. He turned and ran down the hallway to the kitchen.

Shit.

The phone lay off its hook at the end of the dining table. Looking down at the chair, Pete flinched, its off-white upholstered cushion stained with drying blood.

"Fuck..."

Pete spun, confused, looking at the clock on the wall. He ran to the sink's window and looked out to the darkening backyard, the sun below the horizon.

"What time is it, little soldier? God, how long have we been gone?"

Pete didn't want to know.

Greamer. He took them.

Pete scrambled in the kitchen, opening the cupboard, checking drawers, not knowing what to look for. He grabbed the phone from the table and held it to his ear, pounding his finger on the hook like a jittery game show contestant, his body shaking as he dialed.

"She's at her sister's. She's just at her sister's. Come on, Donna, pick up..."

Pete listened to the phone ring six, seven, eight times...

"They're not there --"

Pete slammed the hook for a dial tone and dialed another number. It rang once.

"Yes, hello, I need to speak to Naylor..."

Pete hunched over the table, holding himself up with his arm.

"Who is this? I'm looking for Naylor..."

I walked to the kitchen and sat at attention next to my favorite place under the dining table. Pete was going to need me more than ever.

"Accident? What accident? Who?"

Pete rubbed the dining chair and held his hand in front of his face, staring at the flaked blood on his fingertip.

"Durante? When?"

Pete wiped his finger on his fatigues and shouted into the phone.

"Two days ago?"

Two days? How can it be two days?

Pete screamed into the phone, demanding answers to questions he didn't know how to ask.

"What do you mean two days ago?"

Pete tried to sit down but couldn't bend his knees. He wiped the sweat from his brow with the back of his hand.

"*Mercy...*"

Pete pulled the note from his vest pocket and flattened it on the table.

Wait…

Staring at the note through tears, he rearranged the letters in his mind. His heart, if it were beating, would have stopped.

– – – – –

MORE MERCY GONE

– – – – –

Oh my God. Bea --

It had dawned on him.

EMERGENCY ROOM.

CHAPTER TWENTY-THREE

THICK UNEASINESS crowded the emergency room's lobby with people brought together only by timing. A grandfather in pajamas, a gum-chewing woman biting her fingernails, another man re-wrapping his hand with a bloody rag. All waited on hard chairs, eyes to the floor, situated with as much distance as possible between themselves and others.

A middle-aged receptionist, her pretty eyes desensitized from years of producing order from trauma, sat behind a check-in counter with no line as Pete's muddied body tumbled into the lobby.

"Can I help you, sir?" The receptionist looked up, on auto-pilot. Cold, yet competent. "Are you hurt?"

"Where is she? My --"

Pete crashed against the counter, his bare forearm smearing mud across a sign-in sheet bound to a clipboard.

"Beatrice," Pete continued. "My wife. Where is she?"

The receptionist's eyes siphoned names from the stack of paper in front of her with the tip of her pen.

"What was the patient's name, sir?"

"Durante. *Beatrice* Durante."

The receptionist looked up.

"Mrs. Durante was brought in this afternoon. Who are you, sir?"

"Who am I?" Pete slammed his palms on the counter. "I'm her husband. I was told she's here --"

A woman's screams echoed from the facility's corridors beyond the far side of the office as uniformed hospital clerks went about their business.

"That's... that's her voice..."

Pete closed his eyes, leaning over the counter like a man trying to hear a feather hit the floor.

"That's Bea..."

The receptionist picked up the phone and dialed. "One moment, sir."

That's her. That's Beatrice --

The receptionist spoke into the phone below the not-so-distant screams. "It's Edith. Can you come up here right now? I have a situation..."

Pete opened his eyes.

"Let me back there." *Beatrice.*

The receptionist ignored him, whispering into the phone. "He claims to be her husband..."

"What's going on back there?"

Pete strode to a closed door on the wall to the left of the counter, grabbing the handle with a hard turn. Locked.

I need to be with her --

Pete shook the door by its handle like a new prisoner testing the lock.

"LET ME IN," he shouted. "NOW."

The receptionist stood and leaned over from behind the counter, holding the phone to her ear. Patients in the lobby withdrew into themselves, startled by the scene.

"Sir, please have a seat. Somebody will be right with you."

They all work with Greamer.

Pete slammed the meat of his gaveled fist against the locked door, her screams searing through his brain like white-hot iron rods. He shouted.

"LET ME TALK TO GREAMER. OPEN THIS GODDAMN DOOR --"

Pete turned and faced the room of frightened patients, all watching what appeared to be a lunatic. A black-clad pale man sitting in the far corner looked up from his magazine and made eye contact with Pete.

"WHAT THE FUCK ARE YOU LOOKING AT???"

Pete screamed a monsoon of misdirected expletives into the barren desert of faces and turned back to the receptionist. Reaching over the counter, he yanked the phone from her hand and pulled it from the jack.

"Sir!"

The receptionist stepped back from the counter, jarred, emotions on a time delay. Her hardened hazel eyes became filled with a controlled fear they hadn't known since college.

"OPEN THIS DOOR, LADY!!! WHERE'S GREAMER???"

The screams from the corridor beyond the office walls began to curdle Pete's blood.

"Sir," the receptionist forced, "I need you to please take a seat --"

Fuck this.

Pete swiped his arm across the counter like an angry python, the clipboard skirting across the room. He jumped up on the counter toward the receptionist, throwing his weight into the office, his muddy boots destroying the paperwork on her desk. Stumbling over her chair, he charged at her. She backed away, hollering for help.

"Security!"

Pete scrambled by the receptionist and the other stunned office workers. Touching no one, he plowed through an open doorway and into a hallway beyond the office, drawn to the source of the screams.

Beatrice --

Pete sprinted down a dark ribbed corridor filled with the hanging smell of rubbing alcohol, his moist boots squeaking on the sanitized floor like two angry beasts rushing to save their outnumbered cubs.

"SAVE THE BABY!!!" Her screams hurried along what seemed like miles of walls. "THE BABY --"

Icy hot light and her screams splashed from under a closed operating room's door at the end of the hall. Pete skidded to a stop and threw his body at the door, reaching for the handle.

BOOM --

A stocky male nurse emerged from the hall's darkness, blocking the operating room's door like a defensive tackle. Pete bounced back, blindsided.

"I can't let you in here, my friend." The stocky male nurse sandwiched himself between Pete and the door. "Who are you?"

WHO AM I???

Pete wrestled with the man on his feet, leaning into the door, grappling for control of the handle. Beatrice's screams shot across the floor and into his boots, ricocheting up to his spine.

"WHO AM I???"

Pete's screams harmonized with Beatrice's in a duet of horror.

"WHO THE FUCK ARE YOU??? WHERE'S RIP GREAMER???"

Pete put an elbow to the jaw of the stocky male nurse and twisted the door handle, forcing his body into the operating room. He froze in the doorway and squinted, paralyzed by what he saw. A lidded pail, labeled *BIOHAZARD*, pushed flush against the wall...

Jesus.

She arched her back on the hard gurney, her bare legs hoisted in the air. Doctors with bloody gloves scrambled as the sound of her pain filled the chamber of concrete walls.

"OH GOD!!!" she screamed. "SAVE THE BABY!!! SAVE THE BABY!!! SAVE..."

Pete's knees buckled, the weight of the stocky male nurse and two other large men pulling his shell to the floor. His shoulders hit bottom like two fighting anchors.

"GET OFF ME, MOTHERFUCKER!!! BEA --"

Pete kicked, pushed, pulled, flailed. The men were emotionless machines, braiding his arms back, knuckles to shoulder blades. Flattening Pete out on the floor, the stocky male nurse buried his knee into the small of his back, injecting a loaded syringe into his thigh.

Cheek to the floor, Pete screamed with what he had left.

"NO!!!" *YOU SON OF A BITCH --*

Pete's screams dropped from the duet. Her screams drowned in the sound of his panic.

LET ME GO!!! BEATRICE!!! WHERE'S GREAMER???

The heels of Pete's muddy boots slid like the rudders of a hijacked ship as the small army of men dragged his body across the corridor. They entered an enclosed space no bigger than a large walk-in closet, lined with shelves holding medicines and supplies. Used buckets and mildewing mops took their breaks in the corners of the small room, smelling of ammonia.

Let me up.

Pete's back stuck to the floor of the supply room, his limbs no longer in the game. The stocky male nurse checked Pete's vest pockets for identification.

Let me...

The receptionist entered the supply room from the main hall and closed the door. Beatrice's screams dampened behind its whispering slam.

"He claims to be her husband," the receptionist said.

I AM!!! I AM HER HUSBAND!!!

"The nuchal cord situation in Room Eleven," she continued. "Critical fetal distress. Brought in today."

WHO THE FUCK ARE YOU PEOPLE???

Beatrice's muted screams continued from the hall on the other side of the supply room's door.

WHERE'S RIP GREAMER???

Pete tried to kick, struggling to keep his eyelids from falling like iron curtains.

"The baby has the umbilical cord wrapped around its neck," the receptionist said. "If she doesn't stabilize, we'll lose them both."

NO!!! BEATRICE!!!

"There's nothing on him," the stocky male nurse said, checking the last of Pete's pockets. "He'll be down for a while. I'll stay here with him until he comes to."

BEA...

"What a psycho," the receptionist said. "He jumped over the counter in front of everybody. We've called the authorities."

"And he says he's the woman's husband?"

"He can't be Mrs. Durante's husband," the receptionist said. "I spoke with her sister today. Apparently Mrs. Durante had a nervous breakdown earlier this week."

HER SISTER??? WHERE'S DONNA??? LET ME TALK TO DONNA!!!

Pete's screams never left his head.

WHERE'S DONNA??? BEA...

The receptionist explained, her whispers shrouding Beatrice's lone screams.

"Mrs. Durante collapsed after learning her husband died in an accident. She went into early labor today with the complications."

Pete almost came out of his skin.

BUT I'M ALIVE!!!

CHAPTER TWENTY-FOUR

UNDER THE SURFACE of the earth we went, moving like rats through a tomb-like maze of angled corridors, chambers, and halls. Pete reached into his vest pocket as we came to a fork in the tunnel, its floor littered with debris.

"Hold up, little soldier."

Pete squatted and unrolled the large map, flattening it out on the floor's rubble. He examined the blue ink lines with his fingertips.

"Check it out, Perrier. We're here."

Mag crouched down beside him, reading the map.

"*Triad of Hell*," Pete said, pointing to a large room at the far top edge of the paper. "He's taking us to the library."

Pete rolled up the map and got to his feet.

"Left. Let's go, little soldier..."

Pete and Mag trailed me down a sloping shaft toward the rising smell of tin, passing a series of open doorways in the tunnel's right wall.

"Supply rooms," Mag said, shining his light through the doors.

"Straight."

The passage leveled off, spilling us into a large mess hall. A make-line of steel serving trays took up two adjacent walls of the large cafeteria-like space, with dishes and silverware still stacked on wheeled carts. I took a quick inventory of the hall under its grid of dining tables, some still left uncleared of their mold-coated dishes.

"Chow Hall."

Mag walked behind the make-line, shining his light along shelves of canned food. Picking a hanging ladle off its hook, he slammed it against the steel counter, the metal-on-metal ruckus echoing through the hall.

Tap-tap-tap BANG! BANG! BANG! Tap-tap-tap BANG! BANG BANG!

"SOS, brother. Morse code."

Tap-tap-tap BANG! BANG! BANG! Tap-tap-tap BANG! BANG BANG --

"Let's go," Pete ordered.

We entered a large recreation room just off the mess hall. Tables with scattered playing cards and board games stood pushed against tiled walls, surrounding a dust-covered pool table in the center of the room.

"Over there, little soldier..."

The opposite door led to an airy lobby set up like an underground courtyard, its arched ceiling twice as high as that of the recreation room. Vines dangled from the ceiling like nooses, with smaller rooms spidering out from the main mother hall.

Pete read the map in his hands as we walked.

"Library's on the other side of the barracks. Straight through, little soldier."

I padded across the slab floor to the far end of the lobby, taking us through an arched doorway and into the mouth of a descending stairwell.

"You're the dog," Mag praised. "You're the key."

I counted thirteen steps twice before reaching the flat floor of a narrow room with a low ceiling. Living quarters. Plain wooden bunks were arranged in perfect formation, with each uniformly accompanied by a footlocker.

"Bingo," Pete said, looking at the map. "The library's through here."

The place still looked lived in. Tools of warfare lounged atop the bunks, with miscellaneous belongings tucked away into private corners of the footlockers. Bags and pouches, decks of cards, toiletries, tin cups, helmets, even firearms.

"Check under the beds," Pete said.

Pete and Mag began inspecting the cots, pulling up the mattresses. I hurried past the long row of bunks toward the dark doorway on the opposite end of the room, devouring the smell of otherness through my nostrils.

"*Follow the dog*, Perrier..."

I led us to a room with a vaulted ceiling of stone. A library. Plain rotting wooden tables were arranged in perfect formation, with bookshelves scaling the walls. I stopped next to a ladder on wheels.

"Check him out," Mag said, excited. "He knew the whole time."

"Good job, little soldier."

Pete adjusted his headlamp and climbed the ladder, reading the spines of the books on the top shelf.

"Bingo."

Pulling a bulky book from the top shelf with both hands, Pete climbed back down the ladder and placed it on a table with a thump. The book was the size of a large dictionary, bound in black leather, with a title burned into the cover:

TRIAD OF HELL

"This is it, Perrier. *Triad of Hell.*"

Pete opened the book and flipped through its parchment-like pages under his headlamp. Mag towered over his shoulder.

"Code book," Pete said. "The runic alphabets..."

Pete spun the book on the table and pointed to two jagged lightning bolt designs embossed into the leather spine.

"The *SS* badge, man. Nazis. *Angled runes*, indeed."

Pete flipped to a page of graphic symbols. Some looked like logos, others looked like simple stick figures or hieroglyphics. All were composed of mostly straight black lines.

"The Nazis were fascinated with runes," Pete said. "A German mystic named Guido von List wrote a book about rune secrets before the first war. The Nazis were his biggest fans."

Pete wiped his lips with his forearm.

"Makes perfect sense that Greamer's into this shit. Or it's into him."

Pete pointed to symbols on the yellowing page, identifying them out loud like an old man remembering faces in his high school yearbook.

"This one means *life*. This one means *fear*. This one means *ice*."

Pete's headlamp flickered. He slapped his head, the light splashing on the page.

"Notice the straight angled lines," Pete continued. "Some runes look a lot like our *A*, our *N*, our *X*, our *Z*..."

"They look like caveman drawings, brother."

Pete turned the page.

"Runes go back about two thousand years," Pete said. "Before the Latin alphabet. But you still find them today in modern witchcraft, black magic..."

Mag took a knee beside Pete and looked at the angled symbols on the page. One symbol looked like a stick figure fish standing on its tail, another looked like a bent cross. "Rifle crosshairs..."

Pete turned to the next page and pointed to three cross symbols at the top. The first, labeled *Greek Cross*, looked like a simple plus sign in mathematics. The second, labeled *Roman Cross*, looked like a traditional Catholic cross. The third, labeled *Runic Cross*, was a more elaborate cross, with its four sections interlocking in the middle.

"Look close," Pete said, pointing to the Runic Cross. "See anything in the center of it?"

"Whoa…"

"The center of the Runic Cross is a swastika," Pete said. "The hooked cross."

The twosome examined the Runic Cross under the shared light of their headlamps, eyes fixed on the almost hypnotic swastika shape at the center of the design.

"So the swastika's based on a rune. That's pretty creepy, brother."

Pete turned the page and pointed to two zigzags resembling lightning bolts.

"This one's the *Sig* rune," Pete said. "Like the two on the spine."

"*Angled runes*," Mag said, pointing to the double zigzags. "These are Nazi too?"

"Yep. The *SS* bolts. The *SS* badge. *Schutzstaffel* of the Third Reich."

Pete's German pronunciation was perfect.

"And this one's the *Wolfsangel. Wolf's hook*. Started as a mason's mark."

Pete turned the page, revealing the Nazi flag, its black swastika centered in a white disc upon a red background.

"Hitler himself composed the German flag, choosing the swastika from the runes to represent his bullshit idea of the Aryan struggle. The swastika became the Nazi logo."

Pete stared at the symbol.

"It was the most fucked-up thing the human race has ever seen."

"So the Nazis created the runes?"

"Nazi designs were all based on runes," Pete said. "But runes are a hell of a lot older than Nazis. They hijacked the swastika, making it the symbol of evil."

Pete closed the heavy book and read the cover out loud.

"*Triad of Hell*. How clever." *Adolf Hitler. Son of a bitch*. "Let's get the hell out of here."

Pete put the book under his arm, unfolding the map in his hands. Mag snatched the map and studied it. He pointed to a different door at the far end of the library.

"That way, Lucky Thirteen. Shortcut."

I led us out the far door of the library and into an adjacent hallway that smelled something like a sewer without sewage. We walked into the dark as the walls and ceilings became dirt, looking less like a hallway and more like a hole dug out by a large animal.

"Hold it."

Pete held up a closed fist. Mag stopped behind him.

The dirt ceiling led to a black void ahead of us, with wood planks covering the tunnel's floor like a bridge stretching over unseen open space. Sounds that only I could hear came from the earth below. Pete took the map from Mag and looked at it under his flickering headlamp.

"They didn't label this bridge. Here, hold this."

Pete crumpled the map and shoved it into a vest pocket. Handing the bulky book to Mag, he tapped his foot on the rotting wood planks, rattling their dankness with his boot.

"Let's turn around, little soldier."

I could ignore it no longer. Driven crazy by subterranean sounds penetrating my ears at a frequency I'd never heard, I darted past Pete's boots, running down the shaft toward a smell that waited in the darkness on the opposite end of the planks.

"Shadow, no --"

I skirted across the shaky planked floor like a mouse on thin ice.

"LITTLE SOLDIER!!! STAY!!!"

Reaching the dirt floor on the opposite end of the planks, I turned around to face my master, blinded by two headlamps twenty meters away.

Pete stepped onto the planked floor with one foot, testing its sturdiness.

"Careful, brother."

"Stay, little soldier. Wait for us." *Let's just get the book to Greamer, and this will all be over.*

Pete stepped onto the planks with his other boot, committing his weight to their mercy.

"Should hold, Perrier. One at a time. Watch your step."

Pete walked toward me like a man on a balance beam. One step, two steps, three...

CRASH!

The rotted wood planks gave way to Pete's weight with a damp sizzling crackle.

SHIT --

Pete fell with his rucksack and headlamp, vanishing through the splintered planks and into the nothingness beneath.

CHAPTER TWENTY-FIVE

VERBAL CHAOS had replaced her screams. Hurried footsteps echoed in the hall outside the supply room's closed door. Doctors shouted status updates like sportscasters calling the final minutes of a one-point game.

"RED BLANKET! ROOM ELEVEN..."

Pete awoke, eyes shut, his back an anvil on the floor. The supply room's shelved walls spun around a single hanging light bulb. Planets around their sun.

Beatrice?

Pete's pant legs held him down like bags of cement.

I can't hear her --

"You can't hear what's not there," a familiar voice scraped.

Greamer?

Pete rolled his eyes to his brow, looking through his cracked eyelids at an object on the cold floor beside him. A black sole.

No...

Rip Greamer sat on a waist-high stepladder, a fisherman with a fiendish love for his sport. He stirred a cup of black coffee with a knife, bony legs crossing themselves under black scrubs.

"Hello again, Sergeant."

"ABDOMINAL ANEURYSM..."

The commotion continued outside.

Pete's body lay thawing, his eyes scanning the dim room's organized necessities. Wall units kept order for bottles of spirits, jars of swabs, canisters of pills, boxes of packaged ointments.

"I've always loved playing games in the rain."

Greamer leaned forward, the stench of his festive repulsiveness filling the room.

"And it's raining."

"Where is she?" Pete said in silence. "What did --"

"You chose to kill yourself, Sergeant. You cut in line. You vandalized my workplace."

Pete tried to clench his fists, his forearms glued to the floor.

"SHE'S BLEEDING OUT..."

The shouts continued.

"Don't worry," Greamer said, smiling at the door. "They'll be perfectly fine with us. *Under Dad's E.T.A.*"

Pete said nothing, the blood simmering in his gut.

"I disdain pests like you, Sergeant. First you destroy my design, then you interfere with my attempts to fix it."

Greamer stood from the stepladder, his bones cracking.

The back of Pete's skull bolted itself to the floor. "What have you done with my wife?"

Greamer straddled Pete and hunched down, reading his face like a golfer trying to identify his ball in the rough. Pete breathed through his mouth, paralyzed by the stink of the wretch.

"Your suicide was to be *my* design, Sergeant. I take great pride in my design."

"Bea --"

Greamer stepped to the wall and cracked his knuckles, a defender of his own perverted sense of justice.

"My quota, Sergeant."

Immobilized. *What about the baby?* "Let me up..."

Greamer poked and prodded through a shelf's contents with the tip of his knife, examining the labels of bottles and canisters. The sleaze in black turned from the wall and grinned.

"I like to think of my design as my bride."

Design? "What design?"

"I choose who comes and goes, Sergeant. My quota. My design. Who, how, when, where. I have a system to my surgery of demise. I follow my muse."

"You sick fuck --"

"EIGHTY OVER FIFTY! TACHYCARDIA..."

The corridor's ruckus continued.

Greamer laughed, amused, like an entertained scientist about to test the effects of battery acid on baby rabbits. He sipped his coffee and set it on a shelf.

"When a soul like you makes choices for me, my creative work is no longer mine. You are a thief. Robbing me of the results of my carefully engineered plans. Robbing me of my creative expression."

Greamer turned from the wall, riding a passing wave of rotting anger.

"How dare you deny me that?"

Greamer pulled a bottle from the wall and removed the cap.

"Fortunately for me, it turns out your offense was a blessing in disguise. If you believe in such things."

"VENTILATION BAGS AND HEART MONITOR..."

Greamer looked at the door, his yellow grin scorched with pleasure.

"God damn you," Pete moaned.

Greamer laughed at the truth of the insult, looking at the door with pride.

"I only wanted to protect her --"

"Chivalrous! But it's not your choice to make, Sergeant."

Greamer smirked, his long fingers crafting their wrongness.

"Men like you place great value on freedom of choice. Now your choice will cost you *two* souls."

Greamer took a wad of cotton from a jar and held it over the mouth of the bottle, turning it upside down.

"As part of my new design, I've decided to keep the thief behind this time. It's been a long time since I've had so much fun with a piece."

He rolled his ugly stare to the ceiling, vertebrae crunching beneath his neck's skin.

"*Under Dad's E.T.A.*, Sergeant."

Pete's eyelids twitched.

"What?" Pete's usual sharpness was numb. *E.T.A.?*

Greamer walked back to the stepladder with the moistened wad of cotton.

"Think about it, Sergeant. What would you do if you could live forever?"

Pete said nothing. *What E.T.A.?*

"Would it really be so bad?"

Greamer sat down and crossed his legs like a giant mantis.

"You could live to do it all, with no fear of dying. A superhero."

"CODE WHITE..."

Acid gurgled in Pete's throat.

"You're staying behind, Sergeant. But in order to meet my quota, I've arranged for your place in line to be filled by another. Which is the way it would have been anyway. Only now, it will be forever."

Pete squirmed.

"I take it back," Pete said. "Reverse my choice. Leave her alone."

"*Man never reverses his choice*, Sergeant."

"Bastard," Pete moaned.

Greamer smiled. "You have no idea."

Pete fought to keep his head from exploding, pulling out a reserved coolness from the cellar of his soul.

"Take me instead," Pete whispered. "Let them live."

Gastric drool ran from the corner of Pete's mouth and onto the floor. Conquered.

"It's a creative opportunity I can't pass up, Sergeant. Two for one. I see your lovely replacement comes with an unexpected bonus. A bonus for me."

"PEDIATRIC! CODE WHITE..."

My God. The baby --

"It only seems fair," Greamer continued, remorseless. "You've interfered with my design, Sergeant Durante. You've stolen from me. Now you must pay me back. With interest."

Please no --

"Your Beatrice will now fill the spot that you chose to create for yourself. *Under Dad's E.T.A.*, as it were. You can thank yourself for this one, Sergeant."

"*E.T.A.?*"

Greamer leaned forward and glared down, his corruptness eclipsing the light bulb above.

"And then there's that little bonus for me. Indeed. *Under Dad's E.T.A.*"

"What are you talking about?" Pete asked. "*Under Dad's E.T.A.?*"

Greamer grinned, a riddler taking pleasure in stumping an expert.

"You're slow today, Sergeant. *Under Dad's E.T.A.* Don't you get it? I thought you were the best there is."

Greamer almost looked disappointed.

"Come on, Dad. Think. *Under Dad's E.T.A.*"

Greamer sat back, satisfied enough.

"*Dead Durantes.*"

Pete choked on his screams.

"A free soul for me. Your wife's unborn child comes along for the ride. It is yours, yes?"

"*I'M CALLING IT AT FOUR-TWENTY-ONE...*"

Shouts in the outside corridor turned to murmurs of aftermath.

Greamer basked in his twisted delight, tapping his rotted teeth with the point of his knife.

"Lucky me. I may even take a vacation --"

"NO!!! PLEASE!!!"

"A choice is a choice, Sergeant."

Pete squirmed, his muddy fingers beginning to twitch.

"THEN TAKE ME WITH THEM!!! DON'T LEAVE ME HERE!!!"

Greamer's hoarse giggle seeped through his gums.

"I'm afraid you must stay behind, Dad. To taste eternity."

"LET ME BE WITH MY FAMILY!!!"

Greamer leaned forward, looking down with a flat-coated smile. Pete couldn't even tell where one yellow tooth ended and the next one began.

"We'll take good care of them, Sergeant. Forever."

"God damn you. Go to Hell."

"Indeed," Greamer said with a grin. "But that's old news --"

Pete spit into Greamer's face.

"You chickenshit bastard." The tone of Pete's voice turned from agony to all business. "Going after women and children."

Greamer looked surprised.

"We still got the best of you," Pete said. "You call yourself an artist? Artist, my ass. You're no artist. Your codes were weak. You will rot for eternity knowing you lost."

Greamer couldn't hide his cringe. The truth hurt.

"You say you enjoy a challenge?" Pete continued. "Here's a fucking challenge: I challenge you to a rematch."

Greamer's ears perked up. "A rematch?"

"Let's see how good you really are," Pete said. "Let's see you come up with a puzzle I *can't* crack."

Greamer tilted his head.

"I admire your resolve, Sergeant. You're not like the others..."

"But if you can't stump me," Pete said, "You give me back my family."

"Hmmm..." Greamer contemplated, pressing the tip of his knife into the roof of his arid mouth. "Well, there *is* the book..."

Pete laid out the challenge.

"Give me the best puzzle you think you have. If I can solve it, you let them go."

"A very special book..." Greamer continued pondering. "A powerful book..."

"What kind of book?"

"A code book," Greamer said. "The *Triad of Hell*. Something I need..."

"Where is it?"

"It's hidden in the tunnels under Los Angeles..."

"What tunnels?"

"That's top secret, Sergeant."

"Who hid the book?"

"I can't tell you that, Sergeant."

A cop out. Greamer was hiding something.

"I'll find the book," Pete said. "Whoever hid it, I'll find it."

Greamer grinned.

"Before one finds the book, one must find the tunnels. It's a puzzle that can't be solved, Sergeant. I should know. I've tried."

Pete was not intimidated.

"Try me. I'll find the tunnels. I'll find the goddamn book. You give me back Beatrice and the baby."

Greamer considered the implications of the trade, picking his teeth with his knife.

"You a coward?" Pete said.

"I have nothing to fear, Sergeant."

"Then let's do this. Rack 'em up, you son of a bitch."

Greamer couldn't resist. It was a chance to use the codebreaker's mind to retrieve a book he'd been looking for. A source of power he'd been unable to find on his own.

"Very well," Greamer said. "You have your rematch, hero. Fetch me the *Triad of Hell*."

"I'll bring it to you. Then you let them live. You have to promise..."

Greamer took the wet wad of cotton and reached down, holding it against Pete's nostrils. Pete sat up like a mousetrap and got to his feet, stumbling into shelves, jars falling to the floor. He circled the supply room and turned for the door.

"Bea..."

Pete grabbed the doorknob, his clammy palm floundering for a grip.

"Beatrice --"

Pete flung the door open, escaping down the corridor in his lead-soled boots. It zigged nowhere in particular, becoming darker with every labored stride, zagging into twisted nothingness. He screamed.

And he screamed.

And screamed.

Again.

CHAPTER TWENTY-SIX

WET NOTHINGNESS. Pete slithered, trapped in the pit, groping with his fingers for his lost headlamp. The glutinous floor sank beneath the weight of his body as he wrestled with what could not be seen.

The hell? Mud?

He tried to crawl, a cockroach in glue, his eyes neither open nor shut. He looked up, unable to gauge how far he'd fallen.

"Perrier!"

Pete shouted up into the ceilingless void, his voice dampened and without echo.

"I can't find my light..."

Pete's hands sunk into the soft floor as he crawled, his knees like crutch tips in rice pudding.

"Toss me the rope! It's in your bag..."

Pete's hands found nothing but slimy silence.

"I think I landed in quicksand down here..."

"Pete?"

Mag's voice thudded into the gooey pit.

"You down there, brother?"

Pete wriggled on the gunky floor, its cold pulp clinging to his arms and neck.

"Drop me a light, Perrier. I can't see shit down here..."

The chilled stickiness found its way to the bare legs beneath his fatigues.

"Sun's coming up, brother."

Mag's light shined from stories above, its beam swallowed by the darkness, falling short of the pit's floor.

"Gotta take Lucky Thirteen back now."

He's taking the dog --

A blindfolded bug stuck in honey, Pete struggled to get to his knees.

"WAIT!!!"

He tried flattening his body to keep from sinking. *Tar?*

"THROW ME THE GODDAMN ROPE, PERRIER!!!"

Silence.

"PERRIER???"

Just the sound of fear, fidgeting in syrup.

"LITTLE SOLDIER???"

Pete wiped the gelatinous slop from his eyelids, his dilated pupils catching the ringed glow of his headlamp. Still on, buried in the unseen sludge, miles away.

"THE ROPE..."

Pete's crawl to the glow turned into a labored swim as he yelled.

"PERRIER --"

"Time's up, brother."

Mag's shouts dripped down the black pit's walls.

"Lucky Thirteen and me. We gotta go."

Pete writhed, stretching for his headlamp.

He can't leave me down here. He can't take the dog. He has the book...

"I can see my light, Perrier. Throw me the rope --"

Mag growled from above, a man late for work.

"Quota, brother. You know…"

Mag's throaty voice turned harsh.

"Looks like you found *your Triad of Hell* anyway."

"PERRIER???"

I'll be trapped forever. Little soldier…

Pete wormed toward the glowing ring of his headlamp.

Christ…

Slime crept down his fatigues and under the waistband of his boxer shorts, seeping toward his genitals.

"AW, SHIT --"

Pete began to thrash, panting in the dark, his fingernails reaching the glow.

"STOP FUCKING AROUND, PERRIER!!! THROW ME THE ROPE!!!"

Mag's abrasive whisper floated at the top of the pit. "Wait for me, Lucky Thirteen…"

"DON'T GO!!!" Pete screamed. "PERRIER!!!"

Mag roared down with a new dryness.

"So long, Sergeant."

Sergeant?

Mag erupted with a guttural laugh.

"I've always loved playing games in the rain."

"PERRIER!!!"

Pete's shouts became shrieks, his senses boiling in adrenaline, the darkest of panics cementing him to the pit floor. He screeched from the bowels of his lungs.

"NO!!!"

Pete gagged on reality. He was being betrayed.

Perrier?

Pete's mind spiraled in the tacky darkness. *"Perrier,"* Mag had told him. *"My last name."*

Perrier. Mag Perrier. M-A-G-P-E-R-R-I-E-R --

Pete rearranged the letters in his head, imagining the shapes of the ten letters.

PERRIER. P, E, R, R, I, E, R...

Pete's spine curled in a knot.

Mag Perrier. "Mag Perrier..."

Pete stewed in the hole, his imagination turning the letters upside-down and sideways, flipping them, stacking them, rolling them, back and forth, shuffling them, tossing them in the air to let them fall where they may in the abyss of his consciousness.

Jesus --

Pete twisted in the dark, a tortured animal. It had dawned on him.

"NOT AGAIN, YOU SICK BASTARD!!!"

The harshest laugh Pete knew too well fell like jagged hail upon him in the pit.

"That took you longer than usual, Sergeant. I must be getting better at this."

"GREAMER!!!"

Pete wriggled like a grub.

"GOD DAMN YOU --"

Pete lifted the headlamp from the muck, casting a glow across the pit's rippling floor.

"So long, Sergeant!" The laugh was not Mag's. "And well done. This book will be put to good use."

Pete flailed in the dark, strangling the headlamp in his grip, brushing it clean. Laboring in the goo, he sank to his waist. A heavy fork through lumpy mashed potatoes.

PERRIER. P-E-R-R-I-E-R.

He almost wished he didn't know.

MAG PERRIER.

It was obvious.

MAG PERRIER is RIP GREAMER.

Pete held the headlamp above his head, illuminating the forsaken dungeon that contained him. He screamed in horror.

CHAPTER TWENTY-SEVEN

Xylophones played by baboons with baseball bats would not compare to the noise in Pete's mind as his headlamp lit up the pit. Countless monsters lined the walls like maggoty rice, the entire chasm pulsating with subterranean life.

"HOLY CHRIST --"

Pete stood waist-deep in a rippling bed of larvae, holding the light above his head. Termites coated his body and face, clinging to his skin with their mother's slop.

"GREAMER!!!"

Convulsions. Pete thrashed his limbs in vain, a scuba diver trying not to get wet, digging the depraved mucus from the corners of his eyes.

"NO!!!"

Armies of demons raided every orifice, burrowing into Pete's ears and nostrils, gnawing at the scrotum trapped beneath his fatigues. Every limb went into a spasm as a creature found its way under his eyelid, another searching for a home in his anus.

"MY GOD!!!"

Unable to die. Buried alive in a pit of scavenging larvae for eternity. With no escape. And nobody to find him. Hell's womb.

"CHRIST!!!"

An elaborate tower of creatures ascended from the floor at the edge of the pit, molded together like rungs. Pete combated his way through the ooze and reached for a rung above his head, pulling himself up...

SPLIT --

The rung snapped like balsa wood in his fingers. Pete floundered, his arms reaching for the next rung. Pulling himself up from the goop once more, he began to climb...

THUNK, THUNK, THSSSNAP --

The wooden ladder collapsed, a sixty-foot tower of paper-mâché. Pete plummeted back into the swill with the splintered timber, limbs jerking like an over-wound toy.

"HELP!!!"

Fighting back to the pit's edge, Pete swiped through the wall's sticky raunch with his forearm. *Door.* He grabbed the knob and turned, the ravenous organisms popping like overcooked peas in his grip. He pulled.

THHHACK --

The knob fell from the chewed wood and into the crawling soup. Pete split the waferish door with his fist, busting through with his boots.

Bea...

Head down. Pete threw his body at the door to escape the creeping nest. A bull through soggy cardboard.

Beatrice --

Falling. Spiraling. A dirty sock down a laundry chute...

SPLASH.

Shallow black water. Pete landed with a brutal flop, facedown, his elbows hitting the hard bottom.

The hell?

He stood up, clenching his headlamp, shin-deep in the wash, hacking watery slime from his throat and nose. Squirming termites floated around him in the shallow moat like sailors around their doomed ship.

"God --"

Pete dropped and sloshed in the frigid water to rinse away his filthy attackers. He scrubbed his body with his hands and pulled down his fatigues, the wiggling monsters clinging to his bare legs and genitals. He squatted down in the shallow canal and gave himself a furious whore's bath.

"Fuck me..."

Shedding his vest and boots, he blew a trumpet's blare through his nose and into the sprawling cavern. Head on a swivel, he shook the rancid soak from his uncut hair.

"This is just terrific. Fucking fantastic."

Pete took inventory of his lower body with his headlamp, examining every nook, picking out resisting wrigglers from his pubic hair with his fingernails, pulling a lone burrower from his navel. Sopping fatigues wrung into a bundle under his arm, he trudged with his headlamp through the shallow moat and dumped his boots in the rubble at the shore's edge.

Buried alive.

Pete stepped back into his soaked fatigues and pushed his feet back into his heavy boots. Wet vest hanging cold against the ribbed tank sticking to his skin, he fixed the headlamp to his skull and looked around the watery chamber, deceptive shadows riddling the hard dirt walls. His dilated eyes found a doorway, yawning open.

And unable to die?

Pete dragged a trail of drip from the moated underbelly, through the doorway, and up a tunneled stairwell. He spanked his flickering headlamp to keep it on, sprinting up the steps three at a time.

A dead end waited at the top of the stairs, barricaded by steel double doors, with a large steel lever secured at the latch. At chest-level was an apparatus of eleven rusty steel dials mounted in a single horizontal row, like combination padlocks, yet not with numbers. Each dial was able to be spun, one click at a time, through the 26 letters of the alphabet, *A* through *Z*.

"This shit is getting old."

Dripping like a drowned rat, Pete placed both hands on the lever and pulled. Nothing. He squinted at the unfamiliar mechanism and counted the eleven dials, each set to the letter *A*. *One, two, three, four...*

A-A-A-A-A-A-A-A-A-A-A

...eleven.

Reaching into a vest pocket, he pulled out the map, its ink seeping through muddy paper.

Useless.

Pete dropped the blueprints to the dirt floor and patted down the pockets of his vest, his headlamp trembling. He remembered the large book, envisioning its black leather cover.

TRIAD OF HELL.

Pete counted the letters in the title. *T, R, I, A... one, two, three, four...*

"Eleven. Of course."

Pete's shriveled fingertips grabbed the first dial on the door, spinning it clockwise with a rusty clicking buzz, setting it to the letter *T.*

T-A-A-A-A-A-A-A-A-A-A

He spun the second dial, setting it to the letter *R.*

T-R-A-A-A-A-A-A-A-A-A

He spun the third dial, setting it to the letter *I.*

T-R-I-A-A-A-A-A-A-A-A

And so on, spelling the book's title using the eleven dials.

…T-R-I-A-D-O-F-H-E-L-L

Pete took a moment to review his work under his oscillating headlamp, then put his hands on the lever.

"Open Sesame, you bastard --"

He pulled the lever. Nothing. He studied the eleven letters.

T-R-I-A-D-O-F-H-E-L-L

His imagination turned the letters upside-down and sideways, flipping them, stacking them, rolling them, back and forth, shuffling them, tossing them in the air to let them fall where they may in the abyss of his consciousness.

You sick fuck.

Had to be another anagram. Pete's numb fingers went back to the first dial, spinning it clockwise with a rusty clicking buzz, setting it to the letter *A*.

A-R-I-A-D-O-F-H-E-L-L

He spun the second dial, setting it to the letter *D*.

A-D-I-A-D-O-F-H-E-L-L

He spun the third dial, setting it to the letter *O*.

A-D-O-A-D-O-F-H-E-L-L

The headlamp toiled like a wounded firefly, refusing to die. Pete continued the blitzkrieg of spinning clicks, reassigning each letter of the book's title to another dial on the door. He stood back to examine the eleven dials in front of him.

A-D-O-L-F-H-I-T-L-E-R

Like father, like son.

"Genius Nazi bastard --"

Pete pulled the lever. Nothing.

Shit.

Pete wiped his face with his muddy hands.

"Think, Durante. Think…"

A-D-O-L-F-H-I-T-L-E-R

Pete re-counted the horizontal row of lettered dials. *A, D, O, L… one, two, three, four…* Eleven total.

"What would it be? Think, think --"

Pete spun the eleven dials, stopping at a letter for each. Following his next hunch, he set the first dial to the letter *N*, the second dial to the letter *A*, the third dial to the letter *Z…*

Has to be.

He stood back to examine the eleven dim dials.

N-A-Z-I-G-E-R-M-A-N-Y

He pulled the lever. Nothing.

God…

Pitch black. Batteries dead.

...damn it...

Pete took off his headlamp in the darkness and slapped it with his palm. Nothing. He shook it, slamming it against his damp leg. Nothing. He groped through his wet pockets in a panic, feeling a familiar lump hanging loosely against the back of his thigh, vibrating in spurts.

My phone...

Pete pulled his cell from his back pocket, wet but still on, its battery indicator showing its last remaining bar of power. He flicked away a straggling termite crossing the waning illuminated screen. A new text message from Greamer:

– – – – –

CHECK TO STEP

– – – – –

"*Check to step*?"

Pete turned and held his phone like a flashlight, stiff-armed, the steps descending down to the moated darkness behind him.

"Steps."

Pete almost laughed as he rearranged the letters in his mind. He turned back and shined his phone's glow over the eleven dials.

CHECK TO STEP = CHEST POCKET

Pete reached into the chest pocket of his vest and pulled out the empty cardboard battery package, holding it like a soggy tortilla under the cell's icy glow.

"Fucking Mag." *Or whoever you are.*

Pete stared at the back of package, reading the smeared inked letters of Mag's chicken-scratch handwriting.

A-N-G-L-E-D-R-U-N-E-S

Pete looked back at the eleven dials on the doors.

N-A-Z-I-G-E-R-M-A-N-Y

His frozen fingertips spun the first dial with a rusty clicking buzz, setting it to the letter *A*. He spun the second dial to the letter *N*, the third dial to the letter *G*, the fourth dial to the letter *L*, and so on, setting the eleven dials to the same eleven smudgy ballpoint letters that Mag had written on the back of the battery package.

A-N-G-L-E-D-R-U-N-E-S

Pete pulled the lever. Nothing.

Come on, people...

Pete looked back down at Mag's eleven letters, turning them upside-down and sideways in his mind, flipping them, stacking them, rolling them, back and forth, shuffling them, tossing them in the air to let them fall where they may in the abyss of his virile consciousness.

A-N-G-L-E-D-R-U-N-E-S

"Tunnels *under* Los Angeles. Here you go, Greamer."

Pete spun the first dial with a new purpose, setting it to the letter *U*.

U-N-G-L-E-D-R-U-N-E-S

Leaving the second dial at *N*, he spun the third dial, setting it to the letter *D*.

U-N-D-L-E-D-R-U-N-E-S

He spun the fourth dial, setting it to the letter *E*.

U-N-D-E-E-D-R-U-N-E-S

Pete re-assigned each of the letters to a new dial as his phone took its final breaths.

"Eat this, you sick fuck."

He spun the eleventh dial with a rusty clicking buzz, stopping it at its final resting place, and stood back to examine the eleven dials in front of him.

U-N-D-E-R-A-N-G-E-L-S

Pete pulled the lever. The door opened.

CHAPTER TWENTY-EIGHT

Yᴇʟʟᴏᴡꜱ, ʙʟᴜᴇꜱ, ʙʀᴏᴡɴꜱ, shades of grey. Our rainbow. A common misconception is that we don't see colors, that our eyes see only in black and white, or even infrared. Not entirely true. We do see colors, but not your rainbow. Your reds, oranges, yellows, and greens are all the same to us, each registering in our minds as what you'd see as a yellowish brown.

For the record, we find it amusing that our toys are often made bright red, because seeing such a thing on the lawn is about as easy as finding a strip of clear cellophane in a bubbling hot tub. But we'll find it in other ways.

Dogs and humans share the same three senses of sight, hearing, and smelling. For most humans, the sense of smell is the weakest of all the senses. But for us dogs, it's the strongest. While a dog's brain is only one-tenth the size of a human brain, the part that controls smell is forty times larger than that of a human. This results in a sense of smell that's about one thousand to ten million times more sensitive than that of a human. Depending on the breed, of course. Not to bother you with more math, but while a human has about five million scent glands, we dogs have anywhere from 125 million to 300 million. This is why our noses are wet.

Our nostrils are designed to also let us know which *direction* a smell is coming from. And when we *do* smell something, we're not just registering a smell. We're getting an entire *story*. One whiff of another dog or human and we can determine if they're male or female, what they've eaten, where they've been, what they've touched, if they're ready to mate, if they've been pregnant, and if they have cancer. We detect it all. So watch yourself.

And our ears, you ask? By the time our ears are developed, we can hear about four times better than the average human. (So keep your music down, will ya?) While humans have only six muscles in their ears, we dogs have eighteen or more. This allows them to be mobile, which is useful when we need to move our ears in the direction of an incoming sound.

There is a universal sense we have that most humans do not have. We can feel the energy -- or emotions --

of other beings around us. We can feel your courage, your fear, your joy, your sorrow, your hope, your despair, your love, your hatred. While there are obvious advantages to this, it can also be a burden. Our keen sense of emotion is one of the reasons we're so insistent on keeping you people happy.

Pete's emotions were ones I knew better than anyone. Even Beatrice. Since the war, his emotions had gone to a dark place. A deep and personal place, where visitors were not allowed. And while we had done all we could for him, the fact was that Pete had made a choice that was his to make, and only his. Yes, he'd crossed the line. Yes, he'd passed the point of no return. And yes, it had backfired.

But in Pete's defense, between you and me, I can assure you that his fate wasn't entirely his fault. Coming from a family plagued with untreated depression and a history of suicides, one could argue that Pete's ultimate decision was a result of genetics. Yet as a man who endured the psychological trauma of war, one could also argue that his decision was a result of circumstance. Whatever the theory, one thing is certain: Pete did what he did because he felt he had no other choice.

Every ghost has a story, full of complications. But in most cases, the story remains trapped on the other side of the grave, forever untold. My master deserves better than that. I owe it to him to tell his story. I hope you've been enjoying it so far.

I delved deeper into the tangled underground maze, marking every corner, senses cranked full-blast, my most important chapter ahead of me. Earth's fragrance clashed with the reek of chemicals, natural with artificial, divine with man-made. Tail down, tags jingling, I converged on the approaching figure head-on, in the dark, provoking an inevitable collision. Two locomotives racing toward each other on a single track. Closer. It reached from the void and was suddenly upon me, grabbing my collar and not letting go.

"Little soldier."

CHAPTER TWENTY-NINE

ZIGGING LEFT, zagging right, I navigated us out of the underground maze using the map I'd set with my marks. Pete trembled, gripping my collar, his body as frigid as a slime-soaked stone.

"What's that, little soldier?"

We marched up the final tunnel, drawn like wasps to the yellowish glow that waited at its end. Closer. Brighter. We stepped through.

The hell?

Pete stood with eyes swollen open, his boots like bricks on the floor. The supply room's shelved walls spun around a single hanging light bulb. Planets around their sun.

"Hello again, Sergeant. Welcome back."

Rip Greamer sat on a waist-high stepladder, waiting like a fisherman with a fiendish love for his sport. He stirred a cup of black coffee with a knife, bony legs crossing themselves under black scrubs. He read from the large book cradled in his lap. *TRIAD OF HELL.*

"Not bad, Sergeant. You're a quick one. But we knew that. Close the door."

I found a place on the floor near a used bucket and mildewing mop that smelled of ammonia.

"Greamer?" Pete gasped, closing the door. "What is this?"

Hurried footsteps resounded in the hall outside the door. Doctors shouted status updates like sportscasters calling the final minutes of a one-point game.

"ROOM ELEVEN..."

Greamer fidgeted on the stepladder, his bones cracking. He set the book on the floor.

"Your confusion is normal. Time is one of the most misunderstood concepts to those left to linger on the cusp of seasons. It's actually a lot of fun to watch."

Left to linger?

"It's nineteen forty-six, Sergeant. I suppose you can call it a design idea. I've let you haunt this world for another entire lifetime."

Greamer gulped his coffee.

"One possible world, rather."

Jesus. Pete folded at the waist, his hands on his knees. He stared at the floor. *Christ.*

Greamer cackled like a creature of habit, as if watching his favorite comedy for the millionth time.

"How does it feel, Sergeant?"

Gastric drool ran from the corner of Pete's mouth and onto his boots.

"Did you like the *hero hits wedge*? *Where is the dog*?!" Greamer grinned. "And the Enigma machine. I must admit, that was impressive. Very impressive, Sergeant. Thank you."

Greamer rocked on the stepladder.

"I also appreciate your assistance in the supermarket. Nobody interferes with my design and gets away with it. Nobody! But rest assured, those pathetic souls are genuinely sorry for what they did."

Greamer tilted his warped head back and gazed at the ceiling.

"Wretches deserve everything they got. Or, rather, everything they will get."

Pete willowed. Silent.

"NO HEARTBEAT..."

The shouts of doctors continued from beyond the closed door.

"HOLD THE COMPRESSIONS! I'M GOING TO CALL IT..."

"And *angled runes*?" Greamer continued. "I should have known. Under my nose the whole time. You can be especially proud of that one, brother."

Perrier. "You're sick."

"Indeed." Greamer grinned a scowl of disdain. "I am sickened by obnoxious heroes like you. I must tend to my grudge."

Pete shook his head. "By killing mothers? Grandmothers? Babies? Driving us to suicide? Andreas had three kids --"

"I'm an artist in efficiency, Sergeant. I suppose you can say I'm a family man."

"And I was next," Pete said. "Isn't that right, Greamer? Or is it *Perrier*? Who do you work for, anyway? I was next, right?"

"You refused, Sergeant."

"So now you go after *her* instead? What the fuck? I couldn't let that happen. I did what I had to do."

"Silly puzzle solvers. Your interference is no match for the inevitable."

"Interference with what?"

"I HAD MILLIONS TO GO WITH THIS DESIGN, SERGEANT!!! BILLIONS!!!"

Greamer's putrid breath seeped through his teeth.

"You stopped me before I could hit six million. Do you not realize how much planning goes into this? How much of my time you've wasted? DO YOU NOT REALIZE HOW MUCH EXTRA WORK YOU'VE CREATED FOR ME???"

Greamer grimaced, waving his knife.

"But I admit I'm impressed, Sergeant. You and your Allies brought one of my most effective forces to its knees before I could make my numbers. Before my design could be fully realized as planned."

Pete paced around the supply room, fighting dry heaves.

"But women? Children? You sadistic bastard. They did nothing wrong --"

"YOU'VE ALL DONE WRONG!!! The human race deserves everything it gets. Everything."

Greamer twirled his knife like a wand.

"You're all hypocrites, Sergeant. I've never seen a race of creatures spend so much energy thinking up ways to destroy itself. Doing my job for me. Ruining my design. Disrespecting me as an artist."

"Murderer."

"Ah, but death is all fair and good as long as you control the trigger. Is that not true, Sergeant?"

Pete watched the light bulb buzz.

"You and me," Greamer said. "We're not as different as you choose to believe."

Pete spit.

"But hell, man! Genocide? What the fuck --"

"What's the difference, Sergeant? What's the difference between one and a billion? Genocide, homicide, suicide, it's all the same to me. My canvas."

Greamer snarled.

"I choose my own designs. ME!!! Who, where, when, and how. IT'S MY CHOICE!!! My creative freedom. Man's ability to choose for himself is just one big nuisance. My Achilles heel, as you say."

Greamer swallowed a mouthful of coffee. Pete said nothing.

"You choose to kill millions, you choose to throw yourself from a cliff, it's all vandalism. You ruin my design. RUINERS!!!"

Pete said nothing.

"I don't appreciate vandals like you getting in the way of my work. It's disrespectful. It's offensive. An artist's masterpiece is his to create."

Greamer's eyes fumed.

"Now I must find ways to fill an untold number of slots, Sergeant. Slots that you robbed from me. ROBBED!!!"

Pete said nothing.

"You've no doubt seen the creative shortcut I found in Hiroshima and Nagasaki," Greamer continued. "Hundreds of thousands in a matter of days. Genius, if I say so myself."

Greamer smiled.

"You can thank your comrades for that one, Sergeant. A job well done. Perfect execution."

Greamer cracked his neck with rolling pops.

"But that's nothing. Wait until you see what I've got cooked up for Korea in a few years."

Greamer laughed at his own oversight.

"Well, I suppose you already did. And Southeast Asia after that. And did you enjoy the cute little thing I put together for September two-thousand and one? That rotten apple."

Pete pressed his temples with his fingertips. "So what now?"

Greamer grinned a flat-coated smile. Pete couldn't even tell where one yellow tooth ended and the next one began.

"So now I must balance my quota, Sergeant. I must salvage my design."

"But --"

"LET ME FINISH!!!"

Greamer straightened.

"I find it ironically fitting that you and your Allies provided me with the first replacements. The very ones that interfered with my business in the first place. Poetic justice, as it were."

Pete circled the room, about to vomit.

"But you, Sergeant. You *chose* to jump. On your own terms. Did you really believe I wouldn't catch you? I didn't think a man as sharp as you could be so foolish."

"But what difference does it make to you how we die?"

"IT IS THE PRINCIPLE, SERGEANT!!!"

Greamer stood from the stepladder.

"IT IS MY MASTERPIECE TO CREATE!!! NOT YOURS!!!"

"I was protecting --"

"THE PRINCIPLE!!! I CANNOT AND WILL NOT ALLOW OTHERS TO INTERFERE WITH MY WORK!!!"

"I was protecting my family," Pete said.

"A real hero," Greamer scoffed. "Or even better. How does it feel to be an *angel*, Sergeant? An *angel*?"

"ROOM ELEVEN..."

"I can't say you're not effective at what you do, Sergeant. You don't make my work easy."

Pete looked at the door.

"This is bullshit. You told me this game would be over if I found your code book --"

Pete pointed to the *TRIAD OF HELL* on the floor.

"I know what I said, Sergeant. I'm not one to overlook such details."

"Well, I found your goddamn code book. Now what about our deal?"

"WE'VE GOT A HEARTBEAT!!! RESUME COMPRESSIONS!!!"

Greamer laughed and looked at the door.

"Like it or not, Sergeant, I'm a man of my word. So to speak. There are rules I must follow."

"PUSH MORE E.P.I!!!"

"I must admit. You're the best I've seen."

"RESUME COMPRESSIONS!!!"

"Your intellectual prowess comes with a special bonus, Sergeant."

And then we heard it.

"A bonus for you," Greamer said. "Two for one."

A baby's first cries of life erupted from the hall outside.

Beatrice --

Pete grabbed the doorknob, his clammy palm floundering for a grip. Greamer snickered.

"One moment, Sergeant. Then you must come with me."

Pete flung the door open, sprinting down the corridor in his slosh-soaked boots. He zigged somewhere in particular, zagging to dodge two female nurses leaving Room 11.

"How's the mother?" the first nurse asked. "Her sister is in the lobby."

"Stable," the second nurse replied, carrying a crying infant wrapped in a small blanket. "She'll meet her new daughter within a couple days..."

Pete stepped from the corridor into the stillness of Room 11. Our Beatrice rested, eyes closed, her steady breathing a sobering reminder of time. He went to her.

"Bea..."

Pete brushed a lock of damp hair from her forehead and held her hand in his.

"Peter --"

"I'm here, love."

Beatrice spoke no louder than a whisper. "It took you."

Pete failed to swallow, squeezing her fingers.

"And the baby --"

"No," Pete whispered. "She's with the nurses. Safe and sound. She's fine!"

"A girl --"

"You're going to meet her real soon," Pete said. "Donna's here too."

Beatrice's eyelids quivered. "I knew you were right. A girl."

"A perfect little girl." Pete beamed. "She's going to grow up to be strong and beautiful. Just like you."

Beatrice stirred comfortably with a lucid smile. She exhaled, whispers turning to speech.

"I want her to be smart like her daddy."

"And you can give her the name we came up with."

Pete wiped the snot dripping from his nose, choking on words.

"After your grandmother."

Beatrice giggled in a playful slumber. "Okay."

"Sergeant Durante..."

Greamer stood in the doorway.

"It's time, Sergeant."

Pete released her hand and turned from the gurney, looking down at me waiting by his feet.

"Right --"

Pete took a knee and gripped the roots of my ears, putting his nose to mine. He looked through my eyes and straight at my soul.

"This is it, little soldier."

Then came the orders.

"You are my eyes now. My ears. My mind. My heart. All of my senses. Like we talked about. You hear me?"

Loud and clear.

"It's your shift," my master continued. "I need you to look after our girls. You're the man of the house now. You got a problem with that?"

Nope.

"Of course you don't. You're my little soldier."

Pete stood and took Beatrice's hand once more, pressing his lips against her forehead. He kissed each of her closed eyelids, inhaling her earthly scent for the last time.

"I'll always be here, love. Always."

Beatrice's face shined with peace, her eyes neither open nor closed.

"You look so handsome."

"Sergeant, please!" Greamer had run out of patience. "My quota. You wouldn't want me to alter my design again."

Pete paused.

"Can I stay?"

"No," Greamer said. "Suicide is irreversible."

"Then I'm ready to go."

Pete kissed Beatrice's red lips and whispered into her ear.

"I love you."

EPILOGUE

I LIVED A LONG, full, happy life, and if I had to do it again, I wouldn't change a thing. I took my job very seriously as the man of the house, and, as my master had ordered, I watched over our girls.

The first year was the hardest for Beatrice. I'd lie in Pete's spot on the bed at night, waiting for her to sleep, and when she did, I'd listen to her dream. Her sister Donna stayed with us a lot during those first several months, sleeping in Pete's spot. On those nights, I'd take my place on the floor next to Alice's bassinet. Our Alice.

In the years that followed, my Beatrice and I would keep each other company for hours on end, and the two of us shared many magical moments together. We both heard our Alice utter her first word (she tried to say "Shadow", but it came out "Dodo"), and we both watched her take her first step. (It was actually the third. Alice took her first two steps for me when Beatrice wasn't looking.)

Alice and I had our own connection too, spending my golden years doing the things a dog and his little girl do together. She would pull my ears, smuggle pieces of bologna to me from the refrigerator, and sneak out of bed on dark mornings to sleep with me on the kitchen floor. Every week I'd watch my Alice get taller, growing to be strong and beautiful, just like her mother. It will always seem way too soon.

Alice eventually made other friends, and would have them over on weekends. I watched them play the kinds of games little girls play, like jacks, jump rope, hopscotch, Slinky, Mr. Potato Head, and a couple extremely confusing games called Mother May I and Simon Says. Occasionally the girls would dress me up like a buffoon, covering my head with banana peels, paper hats, and anything else they could find. It was pretty humiliating for a man of the house like myself, but watching Alice laugh made it all worth it.

Alice was born smart. Almost frighteningly smart. Just like her father. She made it to the National Spelling Bee in the third grade, requiring her and Beatrice to leave me with her Aunt Donna for a week while they traveled. Alice came home with an award -- a shiny golden trophy in the shape of a goblet -- with her name engraved on it. Years later, her natural academic skills made it possible for her to attend her favorite college, where she learned many important things. By late January of 1969, after becoming crossword puzzle state champion, Alice would meet somebody special, and go on to live a life far beyond her already bright future. This would all be a great source of pride to Pete.

In the spring of 1954, when Alice was still just eight years old, Beatrice took me to a new veterinarian. A friendly, gentle man named Dr. Wakayama. His hands were cool and soft, smelling of soap, and he spoke with a deep voice that reminded me of Pete. While I historically never liked visiting the vet, I liked Dr. Wakayama very much. He was the one who would make the pain go away.

Dr. Wakayama found monsters in my chest that wanted to take my life, and it had become necessary for Beatrice to take me to see him more frequently. Don't tell them this, but between you and me, there were a few times where I would play hooky, hamming it up a tad so that we could go see Dr. Wakayama. He had a way of making Beatrice smile, and that made me very happy.

The truth is that I was getting old, and it was becoming clear to me that I would not be able to perform my job as the man of the house forever. It was getting close to my time to go, and it was my duty to find a capable replacement. I knew in my heart that Dr. Wakayama was the one. Pete would agree.

Dr. Wakayama married Beatrice when Alice was ten. He loved Alice as much as any man could love a daughter, and the three instantly became a family unit. This made me and Pete very pleased. Dr. Wakayama insisted that Alice keep her surname, and invited her to call him Doc. And Doc he was.

It all ended for me on a Friday afternoon in the fall of 1957. I'd been in a state of pained numbness for months, and the lumps in my chest had gotten bigger. Doc had been giving me special medicine to kill the pain, but it made me very tired. I'd spend most of my days in an artificial slumber.

Doggone it. Not again.

I awoke in the kitchen, wet, my urine soaking through my bed to the linoleum floor. Beatrice was running errands, Doc was at work, and the welcome sound of Alice's footsteps greeted me from the front porch. Watching my Alice walk through the door after school was my favorite moment of the day.

"I'm home, Dodo."

Alice rushed through the unlocked door and into the kitchen, looking down to see me lying in my own sick.

"Oh no --"

She placed her study books on the kitchen table.

"My poor boy..."

Alice squatted down and caressed my ears, as she'd always do. She scratched my belly and felt my lumps.

Behind you, Alice!

I tried to bark, but failed.

Intruder!

Alice had left the door open, and somebody had followed her in. There was nothing I could do but lick her hand as she nuzzled behind my ears.

"It's okay, Dodo. I'll clean you up in a jiffy --"

"Is your dog hurt?"

Startled, Alice got to her feet and turned toward the table.

"I've been watching you walk home for a while. You look like fun."

A boy much too old for school stood at the kitchen table in a grown man's body, with a white T-shirt and blue jeans hiked up an inch too high. He had cratered cheeks, doughy freckled arms, and wore too much

277

grease in his reddish hair. A weak mustache looked for a place to sit on a face that would scare a dog out of a butcher shop.

Alice recoiled, clenching her fists. "Who are you?"

The intruder held a stack of envelopes.

"I got your mail for you."

He looked down at me on my bed, his skin reeking of body odor, cigarette tar, and canned beer.

"Looks like the poor fella pottied himself."

The intruder smiled at Alice in a way nobody had before. I didn't like it.

"Are your parents home? Your mother?"

His dumb eyes looked Alice up and down, from the ribbons in her pigtails to the lace in her socks.

Alice shook her head, curling her toes. "N... no..."

"How about your father?" The intruder sifted through the envelopes in his hands. "Wakayama? You don't look much like a Jap to me --"

"Doc's at work. My father died in the war."

I tried to bark, my vocal cords rusted shut.

"The war?" he asked. "He must have been a real hero."

Alice reluctantly nodded. I could feel her blood pressure rising, her heart beating much too fast.

"I should've known your father was a hero," the intruder said, tossing our mail onto the counter. "You have a hero's eyes. Pretty eyes, too."

I could smell what this guy was thinking.

"Was that your Pogo Stick on the porch?" he asked. "I love those things. I have one just like it. I'll show it to you."

I couldn't feel my legs. If I was to protect my Alice, I was going to need help.

"How old are you? Fifteen?"

She was eleven and a half.

"Come with me," the intruder said. "We can go for a drive."

No, Alice. No...

"Mom and Doc said I should never talk to strangers."

"I agree," he said. "But I'm not a stranger. I'm a friend."

He's not a friend, Alice.

Alice shook her head, stepping backward to the sink, staring at the frayed shoelaces of his worn sneakers. "I don't want --"

"Come on, sweetheart. Just you and me. You'll like it. I promise."

The intruder's husky body towered over Alice. She stood no taller than his chest.

"I've got lots of candy too. My dad owns a candy store."

Candy. Why do they always use candy?

Alice winced, pressing her back to the sink. She could smell what the intruder had for lunch.

"And I have a neat new rock and roll record we can listen to. Jailhouse Rock. Have you heard of the King?"

I stared at the intruder from my soaked bed, hoping for eye contact.

"We'll be back in just a few minutes," he coaxed, stroking the ribbons in her hair. "Come on --"

And then, just like that, he did it. He touched my Alice where she wears her bathing suit.

Son of a bitch.

I heard Pete bark the appropriate command from the deepest part of my soul.

On your feet, little soldier. Get him.

Game on. Wrath time. I sprang from my soggy bed with a borrowed energy, ears back, tail down. Anger roared from my gnashed teeth, loud enough to be heard for blocks.

"HEY!!! HEY --"

The intruder screamed and turned toward me, arms out stiff to shield his oily shell from what he had coming to him. He retreated through the kitchen, stumbling backward through the front doorway and out onto the porch. I went in for the *coup de grâce*.

"NO, POOCH!!! NO --"

I didn't go for the throat. And I didn't let go. Mercy would sit this one out.

"NO!!!" the intruder squealed. "YOU DIRTY --"

Dirty is right. It wasn't clean. I fixed him. I fixed him real good. The repulsive bastard would never have such offensive thoughts again.

"NO!!!"

Alice darted across the kitchen and picked up the phone.

"HELP --" the intruder screeched like a cat in heat.

I took care of his fingers. He'd never touch anything again. I took care of that face. Nobody would have to look at it again. With every last drop of life I had in me, I took care of it. I took care of the whole thing. Like my ancestors before me, I did my job. Everything became a blur...

Sirens wailed. Two policemen examined the 180-pound lump of flesh on the porch. Beatrice and Doc spoke with a third officer on the front lawn.

"It's okay, Dodo..."

Alice lay down on her side behind me on my wet bed in the kitchen, kissing my ears and face. She wrapped her long arms around me, her heart beating tightly against my spine.

"You're a good boy," she told me. "It's okay."

I held still for my Alice, absorbing her tears. A thick leathery hand reached down and tapped my ribs.

"Lucky Thirteen..."

Mag crouched beside us on the floor. He wore scrubs from the waist down and an old knit poncho with no sleeves, revealing a dirty cast on his left wrist and a tattoo of two black wings on his right arm.

"Let's go, brother."

My favorite smells grew stronger. Pine needles, ocean air, cut grass, beef jerky, peanut butter, bacon, fried chicken. I marched with Mag up the final tunnel, drawn like a wasp to the radiant glow that waited at its end. Closer. Brighter.

"Well, this is it."

I looked up at Mag. He smiled.

"You're here, Thirteen. Go ahead."

I dashed out of the tunnel and into the light, the freshest breeze filling my jowls. Squinting through the sunshine, I saw him, just a sprint away, waiting for me on one knee, arms out wide. My master.

"Little soldier!"

Like a bullet I ran, the grass a cushion beneath my paws. I left my feet and flew...

"Hey, man!"

The most delicious of collisions. Pete fell to his back, laughing. We wrestled like old pals, and I licked his smile.

"Somebody's been waiting for you," Pete howled with a grin. "Over there, little soldier..."

Where?

I stood over my master and scoped out the borderless perimeter.

"Over there!" Pete pointed to my three o'clock.

And there they were. Mom, Dad, my three big brothers, my two big sisters, my two little sisters, my little brother, my three other little sisters, and my baby brother. Racing from the grassy horizon, frolicking over each other, each one trying to reach me first.

"Ready, little soldier? You ready? Come on, guys!"

Pete lay flat on his back and laughed, surrendering to what was about to come next.

"DOG PILE!!!"

THE END

For heroes everywhere.

###

ABOUT THE AUTHOR

Intuitive Images Photography

JACE DANIEL is a writer and artist residing in Los Angeles. He has an insatiable craving for words, numbers, thought-provoking conversations, unexpected twists, pleasant surprises, fortunate coincidences, simplification, minimalism, double meanings, metaphor, mind-bending riddles, chess brilliancies, genius comedy, unforgettable films, beautiful music, French Roast ground Turkish, killer Mexican food, and hoppy beer. Chocolate can never be too bitter, milk can never be too cold, and a groove can never be too heavy.

For more information, visit http://jaced.com

16340169R00155

Made in the USA
Lexington, KY
18 July 2012